The Great Merge by a Copy-Paste Developer

IRIS CLASSON

ISBN: 978-91-987784-7-2

DEDICATION

I dedicate this book to my colleagues, old and new.
I'm sorry for what I pushed when I was hangry.

ACKNOWLEDGMENTS

To the programming community, thank you for giving me a home, friends, and encouragement.
To my husband Emanuel, thank you for being my number one fan.

1

For all intents and purposes, Leo was doing great. Two months in and she hadn't screwed up even once. She hadn't accidentally published configuration files with passwords and secret keys, nor had she deleted any servers. She gave the industrial coffee machine a high five and whispered into her scalded hand, "We did it, buddy!"

When she started working at Price and Price, referred to as PP, she had two goals.

Start by being present every day initially then gradually transition to remote work until her attendance is reduced to just once a week, preferably on a day when cake is served. The second goal was to not fuck up and steer clear of any circumstances reminiscent of the *unspoken incident*. Turns out, you can never be too insignificant to be canceled. In particular, if your mental breakdown is immortalized in the form of a viral video that made the front cover of *The Sun, Daily Mail,* and the questionable mental health magazine, *The Wacky Wellness Weekly.*

Besides the *unspoken incident*, there were other reasons two intelligent human beings would forgo their tiny apartment in London, the dreary weather, and a creepy dentist to move to a Scandinavian corner where polar bears were said to roam the streets. Leo had listed these with great enthusiasm when she had convinced Jack to move. They were, after all, en route to an early mid-life crisis. So why not make the terrifying decision to embark on a journey towards adulthood. They had jointly decided Sweden was the safest place to do so. It was time to become a proper adult.

Buy a house.

Fill the garage with anything and everything, except a car.

Pay taxes, *a lot* of taxes.

Bike aggressively to work.

Complain about electricity prices.

Vote and then complain about voting.

Maintain friendships with individuals who also complain about said things.

Jack hadn't been convinced. Not until Leo had pleaded a deal. Sweden would be the perfect place for Jack to launch a new startup. Sweden was, after all, a startup mecca, and she would be able to bankroll their lives while he worked his magic on new ideas.

The Out of Your Mind Gazzette-cover girl's unemployability in the UK wasn't a factor.

"That's not why." She had insisted. "It's a fresh start. I have already secured a job, with relocation expenses fully covered. It's perfect for us!"

"Are you sure?"

"I promise. I'll keep us afloat until you get another successful startup up and running. Plus, healthcare is great and free."

The only recruiter residing under a rock, oblivious to Leo's misadventure, had contacted her with *a Great opportunity* for somebody called *[insert name]*.

Maybe he knew.

Maybe he was desperate.

But so was she.

The recruiter asked if she was familiar with C#, .NET and had dabbled with fronting technologies such as The Java Script and Mark-Up, then she'd be a perfect fit. But they'd settle for a pleasant personality and a couple of years of experience in copy-pasting code from StackOverflow. He backpedaled a few sentences later. If she had a personality, then that would do. He was looking for a full- or possibly a foul stack developer, depending on one's conviction regarding the ability to know absolutely everything in the roam of software development and Dev Ops. She had accepted, Jack had finalized the finances for the move, and then the recruiter vanished into thin air like a balloon bursting after being stung by a thin needle in the form of a very popular video.

Elton, the head of Price and Price, reached out to her, offering a sincere apology. Being a man true to his word or, rather, his recruiters' word, he pressed for the hiring to proceed.

"We have private health insurance that covers Preventative Healthcare. As long as you follow the program, we'd be happy to have you join us."

"So, what's next? Technical interview?"

"I trust you."

"You do?"

"I have to," he had laughed shyly.

Hugo sat down next to Leo and greeted her with a nod and a beaming smile.

"It's a great day to code, boss," he said.

"How are the twins doing? Has Juana recovered from the fever?"

As soon as his twins were mentioned, his smile erupted into an impossibly big grin.

"It was just a phase my wife says. We downloaded the app you recommended, Wonder Weeks. It adds clouds to your calendar when the kids go through a phase. And now our calendar is just one big cloud." With a laugh, he presented her with the app dressed in pastel colors. The storm clouds were densely packed, resembling a weather chart that would deter sailors from venturing out.

"I'm sorry, didn't mean to bring you down."

"No, no. There are suns. Look." He zoomed in and a tiny sun shone through. "This is where they learn something after a phase." He yawned, rubbed the sleep out of his eyes, and placed the phone face down on the table.

"So, how are you, Leo? And how is your husband?"

"Jack, my boyfriend? He is all right. Not sending him back yet."

"He works in IT as well?"

"He isn't working at the moment. He's a Stay-at-Home Boyfriend."

"Stay-at-home-dad?"

"He is a startup founder on the lookout for a new adventure. And he takes care of our cat, Lion." She added, "Although the cat would say he takes care of Jack."

"A cat-dad!"

Hugo loved being a dad, something he wouldn't let anybody forget. At least twice a day, there would be a story, or concern, regarding the twins. Usually a concern. There was always something stressing him out. They ate too little. Too much. Talked too little or too much. There was nothing he loved more than talking about his rugrats. Well, except perhaps his passionate rants against the so-called sport of Paddle. In his opinion, it wasn't a sport at all but merely a pastime for middle management.

Leo laughed. "He'd be great cat-dad if Lion let him."

Talking about fatherhood would easily send Hugo down a parental rabbit hole decorated with photos of messy babies. Every morning, Hugo and Leo would assess the latest assortment of photographs as part of their ritual.

"Oh… so what does he do then?"

"Stays at home. Thinking."

Hugo waited for more details, but Leo had none. That's what Jack did. Stayed at home and battered her brains with

4

new app ideas as soon as she made it through the door. To his credit, he was genuinely skilled in that area.

They sat in silence drinking their coffees for a few minutes before the silence became unbearable for Hugo.

"The big one is buzzing." She nodded in the direction of the coffee machine.

They had learned to interpret the coffee machine's status. If a solitary espresso maker was the sole caffeine provider, it indicated that it was a weekend, and only the sales team was around. Those little piranhas never stopped. If a compact coffee machine was present on the counter, it meant that People and Culture, along with a few software developers and their managers, would be in the office too.

But when her best friend, a towering, industrial-sized, gleaming coffee machine, hummed and gurgled contentedly in the corner, it signaled that something significant was happening. A large turnout was anticipated. They watched people pouring in like ants through the cracks of a wall, hurrying to the coffee machines as if it was sugar.

2

"Welcome, everyone, to our monthly Scrum of all Scrum of Scrums!" Elton, the involuntary CEO of PP, spread out his arms, enthusiastically embracing the lack of interest from the pale-faced audience.

Winter in Sweden had not been kind to them, but the torturous lack of sunlight had materialized as frequent breaks, increased taxes, and a lack of facial expressions, which made for a rather boring audience.

"Scrum," Gerard said, barely audible. A dark, scratchy voice, worn out by time and sarcasm.

"You know what they say, you can't spell fragile without agile," Leo said in a hushed tone.

"No fragile without agile." Gerard smiled. "We don't really do Scrum. There's no company who hasn't found a way to backbend into waterfall again." He punctuated the sentence with a whooshing sound, his fingers drizzling an imaginary waterfall. "Torrential waterfall. Scrum is great for generating Scrum Masters. But I'm not sure what else it's good for." Chesty laughter huffed out of him before he turned his attention to Hugo. Wearing a serious expression and staring blankly, he asked Hugo, "There was a new shark attack yesterday in Mexico. Anyone you know?"

Hugo made his eyes big, leaned in and in an exaggerated accent retorted with a question, "Noooo… Tell me, what's his name? Could be family."

"Jose-something," Gerard whispered.

"Yes! Jose! I know him!"

"You do?" Gerard's forehead was glistening from sweat, and he dried it with the back of his hand. "Anybody close?"

"It… is… my… father." Hugo ducked his chin and lowered his eyelids.

Gerard placed a hand on his chest and gasped.

"Gerard, he is messing with you." Leo shook her head. Hugo looked up, all teeth and smiles.

"You are a fucking idiot, you know that, Hugo?"

"Gerardo," Hugo said, with a thick H, "the sharks are far, far away. It's cold here. They won't come here. Besides, I don't know everybody named José in Mexico. Carlos? I know him. A few of him." He laughed a pearly laugh, pinched his thumb and index finger repeatedly, and hummed *Baby Shark*. Gerard was unreasonably afraid of sharks, and Hugo could not let that go.

Gerard and Leo turned their attention to the stage and Elton, a timid little figure in ill-fitting clothes from a no-name brand.

The joke around the office was that it was *a little bit funny* that Elton's parents had named him after an eclectic singer-songwriter. If Elton was a color, he'd be gray, and if he was an animal, he'd be a possum. Not because they are gray, like Elton, but because of their monotonous and sedentary existence with the odd foraging for edible trash. An euphemism for Elton's teenage years, before he declared himself a technical genius and joined his more charismatic brother, Elvis, on an entrepreneurial adventure.

Elton never wanted to be the CEO of a multimillion-dollar company. However, when his brother set sail for the other side of the grand pond and never returned, the aging parents, quoting Elton's namesake, insisted it could be a really long, long time before they found him. Family obligations forced the little possum out of his dark den and into the light. And just like that, he got his makeshift stage in the lunchroom and an audience of approximately a hundred employees who had turned up for the promised food and not much else.

"I hope you are enjoying the spinach wraps from the local bakery. I'd love to have one, but I'm more of a rocket man..." Elton's forehead glimmered under the spotlights as he scanned the room for potential laughter. "And of course, preferably in the company of Elvis Parsley." Audible gasps spread throughout the room.

"Did he just pull a pun about his deceased brother?" Leo shook her head.

"*Presumed* deceased," Gerard corrected Leo with the same hushed voice one would use with a child giggling in church during service.

"So, this is normal?"

"It is, for PP. It's the new normal since he took over a year ago."

"I must have missed the last monthly. This isn't something I would have forgotten."

"They canceled it. You are lucky you missed the SSS."

"SSS?"

"Scrum of all Scrum of Scrums. They canceled it because it was a public holiday. Only sales showed up. They always show up. Vultures."

"And I'd like to express my personal thanks to sales for showing up at the last meeting, ha-ha." Elton's thumb got a tour of the room. Crickets were his only audience.

Lova from People and Culture hurried to the stage, and with heels half her size stumbled as she grabbed the microphone from Elton.

"But before Elton delivers one of his famous speeches," she waited for the audience to respond with muffled laughter, "let's welcome our latest hire!" Without delay, the crowd located Leo. "Leo Larsson, a Swede that recently moved back from the UK. He has taken on the role as dev lead for the algorithm team, and I can tell you he is one of the best developers I've ever met. Head screwed on right." She twisted an imaginary screw and bolt in the wrong direction.

"Did you hear what she did?"

"Yes, I know! Did you see the video?"

"Batshit crazy!"

Leo's complexion changed to a bright red hue as the whispers spread. Lova froze, a tight grip around the microphone and her flashcards crumbled in her other hand.

Gerard huffed. "She! It's she."

"She?" Lova shuffled through the flashcards she had sweated through, the microphone picking up the nervous shuffling of paper. There was no Leo on the pronoun cards. Assumption allowed. That's what they had been told. "Are you sure?"

"Positive," Leo confirmed. She'd be very surprised if she wasn't a she.

"Oh, okay, I'm sorry about that. Thank you…?"

"Leo Larsson. I'm Leo Larsson."

Elton thanked Lova, gestured for her to balance her way back to her seat, and cleared his voice.

"Welcome Leonarda! Apologies for the late welcome. And," he scanned the crowd, "fantastic work on the API documentation. It was long overdue. The customers were thrilled!"

"Dev *lead*?" somebody whispered from a corner. "That's just insane."

Becoming a dev lead had not been a part of the grand plan. Just like Elton had accidentally become a CEO, Leo had accidentally, through pay negotiations, taken on a role she hoped she wouldn't have to live up to. PP had explained that all the developers had the same salary, and because of unresolved trauma, Leo was unwilling to take on an architect role. Therefore, the only reasonable thing to do was to grab a different play-pretend title, *dev lead*, and the pay rise that came with it. Everybody knows one cannot lead developers, and Gerard was a prime example. He could barely be managed, let alone led. The salary increase along with the relocation allowance had barely enabled them to meet the expenses of relocating. The funds Jack received from selling the startup were held in bonds and bitcoins, pending significant tax deductions.

"And now, some grand news. But before I share the news, I'd like to share some thoughts." The crowd moaned. It was time for *The Speech*.

"Recently, I read an article in *National Geographic* about the clothing industry in India. A woman could tell the latest trending colors by the color of the water in the stream next to her home. Every day she'd go there, after work, to fetch water, and the color would change with the season palette. And it made me think. You know, there is beauty in hard work. And it colors our surroundings."

"I doubt that's the underlying message of that article," the vigilante voice from earlier interjected, only to disappear again.

"And I am pleased to announce that our hard work has been paying off, and we will merge with not one, but two, like-minded companies to create the best charging stations the world has ever seen and a greener future!"

"That makes no sense," Gerard said.

"Let's welcome onto the stage, Gregory and Xavier, from Compare the Price and Pricesonic! Isn't this exciting?"

A weak-wristed applause broke the painful silence. Out of the many scenarios Elton had toyed with when he had practiced his speech, a collective lack of enthusiasm had not been one of them. On the bright side, it was the first time they had all agreed on something. With the help of upper management, the Bjorn Borg Racketeers, he convinced the reluctant audience to join in on the applause. Like Moses parting the sea, albeit less elegant and epic, chairs shuffled and screeched to make way for an angelic creature. As soon as it became clear who Gregory was, the gasps spread like wildfire, and the sleepy crowd lit up with enthusiasm and admiration. A flurry of whispers and the rustling of people shifting in their seats chased the audible gasps. In the realm of technology, there was a figure who inspired both awe and amusement—the legendary Gregory Handysone. This tech titan, in a creative moment, had chosen his own surname without realizing it was ripe for teasing. Time and time again, he'd explained that he was both handy and handsome, but that never stopped the snickers.

Gregory waved through the shallow opening in the sea of people, turning around and moonwalking backward towards the stage while shaking hands and fist bumps. Xavier offered embarrassed nods and accepted the weak thumbs-up that some had the decency to offer. When he made it to the stage, Gregory had done his well-renowned victory dance. This dance comprised jerky, uncoordinated hip gyrations with arms lifted, pulsating at the sky. Rumors circulated it had been an impromptu dance, first seen at the Super Bowl when he crashed the main act, but he insisted that a famous dance choreographer had carefully choreographed it, not drugs. It had, of course, been the drugs.

"I know, I know," he began with a knowing smirk, flashing a dazzlingly expensive smile that showcased his perfectly aligned teeth. "You must be thinking we've gone a bit overboard with acquiring all these companies. But trust me, this is all part of my master plan. I'm no shopaholic. My ex-wives, well, that's another story."

The audience chuckled, well aware of his notorious track record of marriages. It was no secret that Gregory had walked down the aisle numerous times, and each union inevitably ended in a bitter, highly publicized

11

divorce. However, his personal life never seemed to impact his relentless ambition and thirst for success in the business world.

He continued, "Now, let's get down to business. These acquisitions aren't just a whim; they're a carefully calculated strategy to merge my power and expand my reach in the technology industry. Each company we've brought under our wing possesses unique expertise and innovative technology that, when combined with my unparalleled genius, will make us unstoppable. This isn't about satisfying a craving for more; this is about me creating an empire that will redefine the future of technology."

"Let's not forget about Xavier," Elton added with an embarrassed laugh. "Our second genius."

Xavier looked up, momentarily confused, before returning his attention to his emotional support device, his phone.

"Thank you for that lovely reminder, Elton." Gregory slapped Elton's shoulder with no attempt to soften the blow. "I'll be sure to remember it when your next salary appraisal comes around." He smiled with tight lips, making it clear he was not joking. Elton recoiled like an outstretched spring in a worn-out mattress and retreated to stand next to Xavier, who kept absentmindedly scrolling on his phone, doing his best to avoid becoming the next target of Gregory's razor-sharp wit. Gregory's audience always came in three flavors. Those that worshipped him, those that hated him, and those that simply didn't care a bit. Xavier hadn't decided where he'd want to place himself, but it wouldn't be in the first group. Not now that he had met the tech titan in person.

"Wow." Anna sucked in a breath. Anna, just like Gerard and Hugo, was a part of Leo's team. A former intern and a radiant beacon of positivity, she consistently brightened the room with her infectious attitude, impeccable fashion sense, and scrumptious cookies that were rumored to have a secret ingredient – pure enthusiasm. "I can't believe it's *him*," Gerard replied with a gagging sound. He couldn't believe he hadn't thrown up yet.

Gregory paced slowly, scanning the room, mesmerizing the audience that identified as category one. "I am, as some of you might have already guessed, your new CEO."

"I wouldn't have." Gerard crossed his arms.

"Because he's an idiot?" Leo scoffed.

"No! Of course not! Because I did not know we were getting a new CEO until our stand-up comedian over there broke the news." They eyed Elton in the corner. "Which he technically hasn't—"

"—Oh, I'm sorry, and I forgot to mention that we have a new CEO." Face flushed; Elton bowed in Gregory's direction before clearing his throat and picking up his confidence off the floor. The few pieces of confidence that he could find.

"I haven't been the best CEO," he waited for the crowd to disagree but was met by nods, "and I'm frankly relieved to return to my role as department head for manufacturing." He chuckled awkwardly.

"I don't want you, lovely people, to worry." Gregory gestured him out of the spotlight. "I'll take good care of you." Gregory looked like he took good care of himself. But rumor had it that it was often at the cost of his employees.

The trio on stage shared glances, and like an amateur choir said in unison, "We are in this together."

"There will be a separate meeting to discuss this in detail, but in essence, the plan is to merge the three platforms. We'll borrow a bit from here, a dash from there, and BAM!" Elton clapped his hands, startling himself with the loud noise. He shook his hands, his palms red and tingling with regret. But he wasn't finished; he had a well-prepared closing question.

"We're going to create a cutting-edge price comparison site. Who's with me on this?"

Gregory echoed, "We!" but Xavier, now distracted by a spinach wrap, did not echo the sentiment. Nor did the audience. The audience members exchanged glances, confirming their eagerness to end the SSS.

With the room almost empty, Elton joined the duo on stage. They seemed unimpressed, their faces deflated. "That went well, don't you think?" Elton rubbed his hands and gave a meek smile. "Postmortem?"

Later, at the postmortem, they'd express their surprise that the employees weren't thrilled about the possibilities, the monetary growth, and stock valuation. Maybe, Elton would suggest, it was because they had no stocks. Physical or metaphorical.

"That's crazy," Gregory would reply.

"Real crazy," Xavier would agree. "Everybody loves acquisitions."

"Merge," Gregory would correct. "A Great Merge."

3

For the third time in under six months, HR, now called People and Culture, had launched yet another 'team rebranding' initiative. With each attempt, the enthusiasm waned, and the ideas became increasingly lackluster. Despite the mismanagement of resources by the company, the teams rapidly had to create new names, logos, and values.

Gerard sighed and looked at Leo, hoping she'd end the misery and the rebranding. He shifted in his chair, ignoring its complaints. Sure, Gerard had gotten porky over the years, but his confidence hadn't wavered. Like an accordion, he had expanded and contracted with the seasons, albeit with less elasticity as the years passed. He hadn't snapped back, not even close, the last season. Or five. He tried to relax, but old habits are hard to kill. He had been the team's lead for years before he decided to follow his doctor's advice and demote himself to a simpleton programmer. Leo had been offered and accepted his dev lead position, but what he had seen so far had been mediocre at best.

"It's up to you Leo. Are we doing the release testing, or are we...?" His voice trailed off as he shifted his focus from his phone to the large monitor on the wall. They had insisted on the largest screen they could find, and it was glowing with all its 98 inches like a 90s tanning bed. It gave them all a slight tan and declining eyesight. They had moved the meeting room table to the other side of the room to compensate for the radiation and bright light, and they sat huddled behind it, shading their eyes from the emitted light.

"Let's finish the team logo first. The UI tests are going to take half a day," Leo said.

Tim raised his eyebrows but pressed his lips together, keeping his thoughts sealed in, not wanting to overstep as a product owner. "You focus on the business side, Leo on the technical side." Easier said than done, but with five teams to manage, he barely had time to attend their daily meetings let alone meddle with the smaller details.

Anna beamed and pulled the laptop closer.

"Here's our final contestant. The wheels! Representation! We make sure things keep spinning," she said in a sing-song voice, her eyes glittering.

"But why two wheels?" Gerard's fingers trailed the edge of the table. "Unless it's a motorbike, I'm not sure what type of vehicle has two wheels. It honestly looks like two balls." He curled the fingers on both hands to form an O each and held them next to each other. "Two *giant* balls." Instinctively, he let his knees fall to the side, the reflexive manspread hidden by the table.

Leo traded a frown with Tim. Knowing she had to play nice, at least until the probation period was over, she stopped herself from making a dig towards Gerard and traded a frown with him instead. As unlikely as it was, Gerard could be a decent accomplice. He wasn't farting rainbows and world peace, but he exhibited a certain flair of political adroitness and had experience with leading the team. She had seen him regulate his behavior to get the team to work more productively, like a social lubricant but for entitled nerds stuck in no-work-all-fun-mode. If she was going to make fun of him, she'd had to be very subtle.

"Shark boy has a point. Let's make this quick. We've been at it for an eternity. Can we decide on a team logo within the next ten minutes?"

Gerard narrowed his eyes at the *shark boy* reference.

Crimson-faced, Anna held up her hands, surrendering. The logo had been in the works for three weeks now, a sprint and a half in Agile-time.

Had it been a distraction? Yes.

Was it a pressing issue? No.

Was it in the backlog? Yes.

Priority? Depends on whom you ask.

The consensus was that the team had to have a logo because of the reorganization. Were you even a team without a logo? How would the other teams refer to you? Like a child without a name, an orphaned team with no birth certificate. That simply wouldn't do.

Anna continued with a steady voice with a hint of anger. "Let me just try some glow. Okay? Let's just make them glow. That'll take attention away from Gerard's interpretation." She masterfully added an outer glow on the layer and exported the PNG. Tim, who only occasionally graced them with his presence, applauded the result with a slow, sarcastic clap.

"This looks great! The glow adds a little extra." He pinched his thumb and index finger before checking his calendar again. "I have to run in five."

Gerard smiled, one of his dimples lurking in the corner of his mouth. "Two glowing balls." He let out a deep chuckle. "Sure."

Anna looked at Tim, who had been quietly observing the entire exchange with a pained expression on his face. *Aren't you going to say something?* Tim gave her a consolatory pat on the back. The initial excitement to create the ultimate team logo had faded to a dying twinge of enthusiasm that was purely a direct result of wanting to avoid release testing. They all knew it. Except Anna, who genuinely had her heart and soul poured into the vectorized project on the screen. Tim had had enough and stepped out of the shadows.

"Are you guys done, or do I have to use my product owner authority?" he asked in a firm but kind voice.

"What authority?" Gerard grinned.

"You don't want to find out," Tim said, a hint of amusement in his voice.

The team fell silent for a moment before Leo spoke up. "We're done, Tim. Let's start the release testing."

Tim smiled and nodded in agreement. "Excellent decision," he replied, relieved that they had finally sorted out the logo. "And you've decided on the balls as logo?"

"Wheels!" Anna squeaked.

"Balls!" The team chorused.

Tim just smiled and shook his head. "Okay, whatever you say. We can move the ticket to the next sprint if you aren't done yet."

Gerard shook his head and chuckled. "No, we're done. I'm actually quite fond of the balls. The Balls Tribe. Has a nice cling to it, don't you think?" He rubbed his chin. "Or, maybe," he paused dramatically, "Jingle Balls! For that extra Christmas spirit."

"For those that celebrate Christmas," he added for inclusivity.

"Move the ticket to the next sprint, Tim. We aren't done yet." Leo took over the keyboard and collapsed the windows with the various versions of the balls. "Release testing. Okay?"

The team nodded in agreement, unsure where in the release they were.

"How are we going to announce the deploy without the logo emoji to match?" Anna asked.

"We'll be fine."

"What if we use cogwheels instead?" Anna hijacked the mouse and keyboard. "In a circle!"

She let out a wheezy breath as if the excitement had pulled her vocal cords tightly with endorphins in a strangulation of joyful sounds. Five cogwheels in a circle materialized on the screen, her eyes dry from the strain.

"Come on! Can we please do the release testing?" Leo massaged her temple.

"Done!" Anna declared triumphant.

"That won't work." Gerard huffed and shook his head.

"Why? Doesn't look like balls anymore, but the symbolism is there."

"Because of mechanical engineering."

"You are just being obstinate." Being obstinate was more of a constant than a variable for Gerard. The insult evaporated before it made contact with his gray matter.

"An even number of cogwheels is going to make the lazy cogwheel turn in the opposite direction. This means that, in a circle, it is going to lock up. We need an odd number for a proper rotation, and, in this case, an odd number of cogwheels is the only logical choice." Gerard crossed his arms with a satisfied grin. Five years at university had finally paid off. He'd be able to ask for a raise.

"Maybe, just maybe, an odd number of--"

"--the release? Please? Can we please release the improved price comparison?" Leo begged.

Anna ignored her. "--an odd number of cogwheels that lock up seems to be the perfect symbolism for our team since they tasked us with an impossible merge."

Gerard rubbed his hands. "Oh my. I like that. I bet the latest The Tiramisu Team wouldn't get it. I. Love. It." Gerard seldom spoke of love, this logo clearly a winner.

"Tiramisu," Tim corrected him.

"Should we add some glow?" Anna zoomed in on the new logo.

"Nah. Can we add rust instead? To represent the passing of time," Leo suggested. "And not doing what we are supposed to do?"

"Speaking of time, are we done now? Release testing, yes?" Tim's frustration bounced off the walls.

"Oh, look at that. Lunchtime. Let's talk about colors after lunch." Gerard slammed the lid shut, stretched, and bounced out.

"No release then," Leo said in a depressed tone, her shoulders deflated. Tim glanced at her as the others cleared the room. From upper management's perspective, it seemed like everything was going smoothly. The team was making progress, engaging in various shaping and exploration activities, and the grand plan was gradually coming together. Leo gave him a quick smile and a weak thumb. She ought to tell him, but it wouldn't change anything.

He pulled open the door with his foot. "It's too late."

"What do you mean?"

"You got to be there at least a quarter to if you want to get the fish soup. The line is probably miles long by now."

"Oh. The fish place. Yeah. Too late for the soup."

"One could say it's their soup-er power." Tim's voice faded down the corridor, followed by a chuckle.

Soup-er.

4

"You would not believe what happened at work today."
Leo kicked off her shoes and picked up Lion, burying her
face in the cat's soft fur. "Hello, my little bebe." Purring,
Lion briefly embraced the affection but quickly realized
that demonstrating appreciation towards humans was
prohibited as per the ten cat amendments.

Leo lifted her nose to the air, taking in the scent of the
strong, meaty aroma that had taken over the apartment.

"What is that smell? Is it you, Lion?" Lion pivoted on
his paws, giving a menacing glare, and hissed his way to
the kitchen, where he would use food to cope with the
insults.

With a pastel pink apron and yellow flowery oven
mitts, Jack made his entrance. He pressed his lips against
hers and made a loud and lengthy smooching sound.

Leo gently pushed him back. "Watch the cheek. Hurts
like hell today. What are you making?"

"Toad in a hole."

A smile played on her lips as she adjusted his apron.
"Too cute. I had forgotten I even had this. Samantha's
farewell presents didn't disappoint."

He battered his eyelashes, embracing the cuteness of an
anime chef. They'd settled on a routine where he'd prepare

dinner on weekdays and she'd cook on the weekends. They were terrible chefs, but saving money was worth the lackluster dishes.

"But what on earth is *toad in a hole*?"

"This," he pulled her into the kitchen and presented a large beige dish that looked like a potato graveyard for sausages, "is the best of the United Kingdom."

"Surely you mean Entitled Kingdom? I love you, but that looks…" She laughed as Jack raised his eyebrows in feigned offense.

"Do not insult British food and its creative variations of beige and brown!"

"You know I will."

"Swedish food is the same."

"No, it's not!"

"Meatballs? With potatoes and gravy? Colors? Miss Beige and Mister Brown."

"We add peas." As a matter of fact, she had even added extra peas the day before. Delightful frozen. Every dish had to have at least a vegetable or legume, and potatoes didn't count.

"Jansons Frestelse? All beige. With *anchovies*. Flygande Jacob? Beige, beige, and more beige. With *bananas*."

"I'm impressed with your knowledge of Swedish cuisine!" She snatched a fork and pilfered a bite. It tasted amazing.

"Well, this is our home now, so I got to get my Swede on." He wiggled his eyebrows and pulled out a chair for her.

"Okay, listen to this!" he exclaimed, bubbling with sudden excitement like a sugar-fueled child. She nodded for him to continue and braced herself. Another app monologue.

"So, the app. The greatest app ever created, mind you. It's called 'Let's get it on'. Imagine this…" He twirled his fingers dramatically, his voice matching the flair.

"Do I have to imagine? Can't *all the people* do it instead?" A puntastic joke.

"An AI-driven app that helps couples, regardless of constellation, optimize their intimacy. Because, you know, the less you have sex, the less it's going to happen."

"Yes, that seems normal. Less sex means, well, less sex."

"No, yes." He thought for a moment. "What I'm saying is that it's hard to get started again when it's been too long. But what is too long? The app will let you know. You input frequency, duration, level of pleasure, and more, and the app notifies the partner, or partners, when it's time again.

She ate on, speechless.

"Cool, right?"

"So basically, a reminder app. But for sex." She fed him a piece of the batter.

"Well. I guess you could call it that," he said between bites. "Oversimplified. Very oversimplified." He frowned, his enthusiasm waning for the first time. He looked around sheepishly.

"Why would I need a reminder app when I have you?" Leo said, tapping on his shoulder. "You know I'm just pulling your leg, right? You've got better ideas than this."

He nodded, took another bite, and lit up. "But you'd probably prefer to hear it from an app instead of me!" he said with a wink.

"Fair point. You should do it. The AI-powered sex-reminder app."

"It doesn't sound as fantastic when you call it that. Sex-reminder app."

"Jack, sometimes fantastic things don't sound fantastic, but they lead to fantastic things."

He took the hint and grinned.

"Well, nonetheless. Now I'm not sure about the app anymore. But I'll add it to the list."

"Which number is this?"

"This one? Number two hundred and sixty-six," he said, his face glowing with enthusiasm again.

"Oh wow. That's a lot of ideas."

Jack nodded, his eyes twinkling. "But this one is the best so far!"

"Really?" Her brain had done that helpful thing where it would erase terrible memories or useless app ideas. "The other ideas must have been really special."

"Are we doing early beta testing?"

"You *beta* believe it!"

With the beta testing out of the way, they laid in bed in a pool of sweat, staring at the ceiling. Lion had been staring at them the whole time. Jack had told Leo repeatedly that the cat creeped him out, even though he did his very best to get along with Lion. And fair enough, Lion would probably not even wait until they had taken their last breath before feasting on them. A dog would just happily sit there for two weeks, panting happily, thinking his owners were taking a really long nap, but they'd feed him soon.

"How was your day?" Jack rolled onto his side and examined the hair stuck to the side of Leo's face. He'd failed to convince her to grow it past chin length. And she had failed to get him to shave regularly. He scratched at his stubble. She watched him with a smile, waiting for him to brush her hair out of her face like he always did. She kissed his hand as it brushed her lips.

"It's official now. We were acquired alongside two other companies. And we are supposed to merge together. Like, yesterday."

"No way!"

Leo nodded and moved closer to him, her chin pressed against the thick pillow. She wanted thin pillows; he wanted thick. Their financial situation limited them to purchasing one each.

"But that's a good thing, isn't it babe?" He brushed away more hair from her face. Her smile disappeared, and her thinking-wrinkle appeared. A deep line between her eyebrows that only showed up when she was pondering a problem. Her face had always been good at communicating, even when she wasn't.

"Now, why would that be a good thing?" She groaned.

"You get to show them that you are a fantastic developer and dev lead—"

"—which the internet has decided I'm not—"

"—And in merely three months, you'll be a permanent employee."

She rolled onto her back and bit the inside of her chin. She really ought to see a dentist. In three months.

"Leo, look at me." He pulled her arm, and she rolled back, facing him. "You can do this. I *know* you are a great developer. Ignore the gossip. Your work speaks for itself."

"I've never seen a successful merge."

"Then this will be the first one. If anybody can make that happen, it's you."

She raised her eyebrows.

"Three months, Leo. You said so yourself, firing people in Sweden is practically impossible."

"What if the other CEOs find out?"

"About what?"

Leo narrowed her eyes. As much as she loved their witty banter, she was not in the mood for it. Not about this.

Jack backtracked the banter. "Elton knows, and he doesn't care. He even wants to help you with therapy, Leo."

Elton was different. A genuine and kind soul, always thinking the best about everybody. That's how her colleagues had described him.

"But Elton isn't CEO anymore."

"Seems unlikely the new CEO doesn't know."

"Elton doesn't seem like the type of guy to bring it up, and Gregory seems rather preoccupied with himself. And Xavier seems... I don't know. A bit lost."

Jack jolted upright, his hands covering his mouth. "Wait. *The Gregory*? One and only?"

"I'm sure there are other Gregories out there. But yes. Handyson." As the syllables left her mouth, she rolled her eyes. An additional minute of tongue scraping would be necessary to eliminate the sour taste from her tongue. Unfortunately, Jack was a Gregory fan, which made sense for a serial entrepreneur. It was easy to be a fan when you didn't have to deal with Gregory and his antics, she told Jack.

"Well, babe. He is not known for being an empathetic person, I'll give you that." He laid back next to her, squeezing her hand. "But let's focus on the positives. You are going to therapy, and more importantly, you are going to do great as a dev lead. I believe in you."

5

Leo had taken it upon herself to reject any recurring meetings that didn't explicitly require her particular expertise—coding and grumbling about not coding.

Just a fortnight ago, she had been lamenting the two or three weekly meetings. However, following the acquisition, the number of meetings and the time spent in them both rose drastically. If this continued, she would soon have a lasting impression of her backside on the corner conference chair. Moreover, free time was crucial for her to oversee and guide the team effectively.

Another dreaded Monday morning and Leo was busy calculating her future. Given the growth of the number and median duration of meetings, assuming two weeks as the midpoint of the S-shaped curve (commonly seen in technology adoption diagrams), when would her calendar be saturated with meetings that total forty hours?

She would need the saturation point for the number of meetings, which was unknown, but she had the total duration constraint that she could use instead. Two thousand four hundred minutes. Forty hours. Calculating the growth rate for the number of meetings and median duration, using the saturation point of forty hours, there would be approximately twenty-six point sixty-seven meetings in week four point nine.

The calculation had taken half a day, but it had been worth it, and she had it time registered under education. After all, she had to read up on all the math she had assumed she'd never need.

There were two distinct species of meetings in the corporate jungle: those led by executives and those orchestrated by dev teams.

Their PowerPoint presentations and long-winded anecdotes could easily identify the former, which made them nearly impossible to ignore. Attendance wasn't technically mandatory, but a word of caution: they fully expected you to be well-versed in everything they said, even if you avoided their drawn-out gatherings.

Using whiteboard tools, diagrams that made no sense, and a general lack of direction and preparation recognized the latter. The meetings would often have the words shaping, exploration, retrospective, planning, and refinement in the meeting title. With no respite from corporate theatrics and agile tango, programmers would go mad from being trapped in endless circles of discussion.

For Leo, declining the invites was nothing short of a desperate bid for sanity preservation. Alas, there was a sinking feeling that it might already be too late for dear Leo. What Leo hadn't planned for was to let every meeting attendee, for the planned three hundred and twelve meetings, know accidentally that she was not attending.

And the email was sent to each attendee. Nine hundred of them. For every meeting planned for the next year.

She made sure to calculate the result.

Three hundred twelve meetings multiplied by nine hundred emails per meeting equals two hundred eighty thousand eight hundred emails. For the first time in her life, she hoped her basic math skills had failed her or that the emails from the shameless meeting-hater had gone directly to the spam folder.

Hugo had called out. It was about solidarity - they'd be miserable together. "Misery loves company." Which would explain why he and Gerard, although supposedly hating each other, never left each other's side.

"And I love to code. I moved to Sweden for this job. To avoid the corporate grind. So yes, while I sympathize with your misery, I'm going to choose to code over meetings any day." Or calculate the saturation point of meeting.

Hugo just sighed in agreement.

"But you should know, boss, rumor has it that they will do an attendance roll."

"Like they did in school?" Leo shuddered.

Hugo chuckled. "Pretty much."

"I'll be there for the attendance call then."

Leo had a plan. She prepared the stay-alive script. She'd be there for the attendance call, turn off her camera as nobody would notice with nine hundred attendees, and then she'd run the script, which would make sure general comments such as *yes! Awesome!* and random emojis would be pasted in the chat, showing her participation. She ensured no accidental peach, water squirt, or eggplant were shared by whitelisting emojis.

She went and grabbed the basket of laundry and tried to enter the meeting. This meeting has reached maximum capacity. *Please try again later.* Two minutes later, she was in.

"Hello! Can everybody hear me?" No replies. They were all muted. "Okay! Let's get started! But first, attendance roll!" Gregory's face filled the screen. His camera zoomed in and out as he bobbed his head, but he remained blurry.

"I thought the meeting wasn't mandatory?" somebody wrote in the chat.

"No mandatory meetings, but we would like to know who is here. Daniel, do we have a Daniel here?"

"We have twenty Daniels."

"Daniel…Johansson?"

"That narrows it down to eleven." Laughing emojis galore.

The attendance roll for the meeting had started off as a simple endeavor but quickly spiraled into a rather tedious process. With nine hundred people in a Zoom meeting, it seemed impossible to get through all their names in one go.

Leo sorted the clothes. Two piles. Jack's and hers. His pile was tiny. He hadn't changed clothes more than twice in the last few weeks.

Hugo sent a message.

```
Hugo: You might want to turn off your camera
as you are folding.

Hugo: Can you fold mine as well? At least
somebody is getting something done.

Hugo: You should try Kundo folding.
```

Gregory took over when People and Culture had given up on the attendance roll.

"Okay, peeps. Let's move on to the first item."

Slide one out of sixty-two colored the screen. Gregory green-screened himself in a corner, but the top half of his head was removed.

"Can everybody see my screen?"

Yesses filled the chat window.

"Fake News number one…"

A stock photo of a woman with a pained expression holding a stack of papers appeared on the screen. "…That we are going to force the software developers to print out the code they've written for the last weeks." Dramatic pause. "Obviously, that would not be environmentally friendly," Gregory laughed from his corner.

The trees were safe. Leo's team hadn't written any code for two weeks. She wasn't sure if she should be proud of their environmental effort or not.

The second slide floated above Gregory's head. "Fake News number two! Remote work won't be allowed anymore." Gregory laughed. "Why would we want to pay for more office space? Stay woke, stay remote!" Gregory had missed the news that woke was not woke. He clicked his way through the slides, and Leo finished folding the clothes.

```
Anna: wanna to see what I'm baking for
tomorrow?
Anna: sorry, wrong chat. But wanna see?
```

"Fake News number thirty-two! We are reorganizing the teams. We are revamping the teams."

Crackling announced an unmuted attendee. "In other news, this ain't Fake News?"

Gregory laughed, went offscreen for a second, and came back with a big smile plastered on his face. "A shake up! I'll talk to you later, Jon." Little did Gregory know there were five Jons, and none of them would admit to the interruption. It would have been fun if there had been an anonymous live commentator. Leo smiled at the thought. But she didn't have the required gusto.

"And the last Fake News..." Gregory did a drumroll. Half the attendees had left the call. Leo had unpacked an IKEA box and had spread the pieces out on the floor. The drawings in the instructions had a little man with a creepy smile that always looked like he was jumping the furniture. It could have been you, Jack; it could have been you, Leo sighed. Jack had declared himself unhandy unless it involved a hand controller or coin empire. "… we are closing an office and firing the employees without a severance, using local bankruptcy as an excuse." That was oddly specific. Gregory laughed, and his eyes darted back and forward, nervous albeit the laugh. "Fake news. That one," he insisted.

"Next one up. We will measure team performance. How amusing! We look at people not metrics, and we recognize performance can't be quantified. We are just going to do some data collection and find some inspiration so we can get the best out of you!"

"As in… measuring performance?" an unmuted voice, assumingly on its last day, enquired.

"Team building with product building." Gregory's smile dropped for a second. He dragged a palm over his mouth, a forced smile added back. "And now for some HR, sorry, People and Culture, information!"

Lova took over and went through the last slides about insurance policies, culture, and values. Only ten attendees remained, one of them ready to log out as soon as she had released the cookies from her prison oven. Nine to go.

Gregory returned, his unrealistically smooth skin glowing on the monitor in the dim office where Leo was busily deciphering the instructions on page five of the humping-furniture-guy-instructions.

"Thank you, everybody, for the meeting. I know we went over a little, sixty-two minutes to be precise, so I won't steal more of your time. Ciao!"

The screen went black. Leo moved on to page six with a firm grip around the Alan key. Are you my friend today, Alan? The key remained faceless.

"I don't think we should have brought up the last one," Xavier's voice was barely audible.

"They are talking about it. We must. It's too soon. We need to buy some time," Gregory replies in a hushed voice. "Did you disconnect the meeting?"

A click sounded. "Yes. I'll close the lid. The camera freaks me out. The light is always on."

"Nell Support is replacing it?"

"It's the last thing they haven't replaced yet on this laptop." Xavier's laughter sounded like wounded geese, and Leo, frozen on the floor, pressed a palm against her mouth to stop herself from laughing at the bizarre sounds.

"I'll get you a new one when we've downsized."

"Any more thoughts regarding which office?"

"It depends on the performance report. But the Sweden office is costly. Never been much for Swedes, anyway. We will see if they are worth the investment. But so far, I'm not impressed." Gregory smacked his lips.

"The laptop is awfully warm," Xavier mumbled.

Leo held her breath. She hadn't assembled the stool past page six.

"Zoom is still running," Xavier whispered. "Hello? Anybody still connected? LL?"

Leo stared at the monitor. Her name, LL, in a purple circle.

"I think it just froze. I can't click on anything."

Gregory clicked his tongue. "I'll find out who LL is and check the activity log. Let's hope it's either frozen or a lazy employee pretending to attend."

6

Aggressively biking through the rain hadn't lifted Leo's spirits. What had used to be a reliable outlet for emotional challenges had failed her. The pouring rain followed her around like a dark cloud concentrated above her head, pelting her face with hefty droplets.

After the Fake News meeting, she had been filled with a mix of emotions. On one hand, there was the dread of having to pay back the expensive relocation fee -something she never expected would come back to haunt her. Software developers were far and few between, and she had never been more popular in her life. If only she had a sliver of that during her high school days. And Jack. She had tricked him into moving to Sweden by promising she'd take care of them while she barely managed to keep her own head above water. And what about the team? Hugo and the impossibly cute twins, grumpy Gerard hoping for early retirement, Anna who had finally pinpointed cake preferences and dietary needs. Compounding these feelings was the uncertainty of whether she could weather another storm. Literally and metaphorically.

She wasn't sure how many of the slides in the Fake News presentation were premonitions versus rumors. Speaking of, rumor would have been a less dramatic word for Fake News. In a world where short-term profits often took precedence over long-term sustainability, investors could be very dangerous. She figured they'd make decisions for the quick buck, no matter how it would hurt the company or their workers later.

She secured her bike to a lamp post, ignoring the *No Bikes!* sign. Bikes were scattered everywhere. Who would waste their time to police a scrappy bike with flat tires? She shook her head free from the helmet. Maybe she was making a mountain out of a molehill. It could be Fake News, like they said. After all, slide twenty-something had been about overtime. "We won't require or expect overtime! Leo let out a maniacal cackle as she took a wide step over the small poodle. *Swedes don't do overtime. We just don't.* She pushed open the office door, a final splash of rain pouring from the ledge above.

"Wait! Would you mind holding the door?"

A pair of burly men struggled with an IKEA bed as they approached the door, followed closely by two additional duos.

"Are you sure it's the right address? This is an office, not a private residence."

Beefy one looked up at the sign. "Yup. This is it." They shoved past Leo, awkwardly pushing the beds through the door.

Leo walked slowly behind them, slow enough to avoid conversation.

"Janet, what are the beds for?"

The receptionist, which also was HR and economy, beamed at Leo.

"It's for our new overnight rooms!"

"Over what?"

"Night."

"Are we expected to use them?"

"I assume." Janet shrugged. "For long days during the merge. That's what I heard. But you didn't hear it from me."

"I'm pretty sure I just heard it from you."

The playfulness vanished from Janet's smile. The joke had lost its charm. Leo's initial excitement about the prospect of sleeping on the job (which she had already arranged by working remotely) dissipated.

"Leo! Everybody is on time for stand-up!" Anna's gaze was full of energy and eagerness. It was Monday morning after all, and she had a fresh tray of vanilla-smelling cookies.

"Hawaiian vanilla," she explained, her tone slightly deflated like an old balloon. "Still can't get a hold of proper black garlic."

"Racist!"

"What?"

"People and Culture made an announcement; we can't say black or white."

"Dark garlic then. But it's not what it's called. Not that I can find any to share with you."

"No damn garlic cookies for me." Gerard pretended to throw up.

"It tastes like rich caramel, not garlic."

He hurled, to which Anna rolled her eyes.

The Kanban board lit up the screen, and everybody confirmed they could see the shared screen and Leo's YouTube tabs with How to Dev Lead. The Kanban board displayed the tickets with things that had to be, should be, or could be done. Neatly organized in columns by their state, they'd pick a ticket on the left and move it column by column to the right until it made it to the Done column. The best column. There were also horizontal lanes across the columns that split the tickets into sections by product type. As per usual, they walked the board from right to left. The Done column had one ticket, but the column next to it, Almost Done, had a tsunami of yellow tickets.

"Anything new in Almost Done?" Leo said with an exasperated tone.

"Yes," Gerard replied but offered no further information.

"And maintenance swim lane?"

Gerard looked at her, his expression one of horror and agony.

"You said swim lane," Hugo said, "you can't do that. He freaks out. Water, starks."

"Starks?"

"We try not to use the trigger word," Anna explained.

"He is no genius; he knows it replaces the stark word. But he insists," Hugo shrugged.

Leo blinked twice.

"Stark. Bark. Lark. Any of those will do," Anna added.

Leo looked at Gerard. He seemed unfazed by the special treatment. If anything, he seemed to enjoy it.

"Okay. Okay. Okay. No stars, and no dim lanes. Testing looks the same. And nothing new in Development. Is anybody doing anything? And is anybody going to take a look at the pull request?"

"I mean, I won't have an aneurysm over a PR that stays up for a few days." Gerard took another bite of his sandwich and wiped his hands on his shirt.

"It's been there for a week at least," Leo replied.

"That's a few days, plus a few more days. Few plus few equals few."

"Hugo, what are you working on?"

"How did this turn into an interrogation?" Hugo's profile picture lit up, remoting from his kitchen office. A chubby baby eating pasta with his body instead of his hands was set as his profile picture. It was either one of the twins or him. "You think great explores work great under pressure?"

"Pressure makes diamonds!" Anna replied.

"And prolapse." Hugo added. "Or hemorrhoids."

"Can you at least add it to the board?"

"It's there. In a separate swim lane."

"Another one?" Great. The board had ten columns and eleven columns, approximately fifty tickets and four different colors indicating different tickets, and priority dots in six different shapes and sizes. It was not a Kanban board anymore; it was a war zone with agile casualties.

"Is it the Shape or Shaping Lane?"

"Shaping. The other one is a typo. It's the Shame lane. We added that one last week for tickets that we are ashamed of."

"Why is Fix Cypress tests there?"

"Because we just increased timeout and hard-coded positive return values."

"But we are being positive!" Anna giggled.

"Are we done? I need to lie down after this standup. As a matter of fact, I might break in one of the new beds."

"Are you heading back home? But you just got here! And I have cake for our break!"

"Oh. You didn't know either." Leo bit her lip. "They are installing overnight rooms. For the merge."

"The Great Merge?"

"Great what?"

"That's the official name for the merge."

"Oh God." Hugo turned on his camera, his eyes dilated. "Tell me about the beds."

Leo filled him in.

"What if the other rumors are true? Maybe they'll close this office and fire all of us."

Gerard woke up from his nap. "That's ridiculous. Why would they do that? We are one of the best teams."

"In *this* office, yes, but not across the companies. Have you seen what the Belgian office is doing? They are more or less launching rockets with Rust. It's so complex nobody can decipher it."

"That's not a good thing," Gerard laughed, "well, unless they need you around to decipher…" His voice dropped, and his laughter ebbed out as he heard his own words.

"I shouldn't share this," Leo rubbed her hands and looked at a very pale Hugo, "but after the meetings—" Leo's phone vibrated. It was ringing. It was actually ringing. That never happened. She had forgotten that the phone could make and receive calls.

"Hello?"

A jarring sing-song voice replied, its tone forced to a higher pitch. "This is Gregory. Would you mind coming to my office?"

"You have an office here?"

"Elton's old office. He won't be needing it now. See you in two minutes?" He hung up before she could reply.

Leo stared at the phone.

"Gregory wants to see me."

"Lucky! One-on-one time with the CEO? He is amazing. I wish I was you right now, Leo," Anna beamed. "Except maybe I'd like to keep my clothes." Fair point. Anna had more style in her right index finger than Leo had in her entire closet.

7

Elvis, the former CEO lost at sea, had kept the office simple and unadorned in the days he occupied it. A wooden desk in the corner, some posters on the wall, and a shelf filled with books that he had collected over the years. And a stack of Elvis Presley CD's, each disc adorned with the King in impressive outfits and bouffant hairstyles. He was adamant that CDs would make a comeback, and nobody could convince him otherwise. If vinyl made it back, then why not CDs?

When Elton took over the office, he left it exactly as it had been, furniture and all. He chose not to alter the room, not out of expectations that his brother might return, nor to keep the memories intact. Elton simply didn't want, or need, an office. He was busy helping his coworkers and collaborating side-by-side, adjusting for differences in stature. He had never been the one to flaunt his endeavors or title, and neither had Elvis, despite his namesake's love for flamboyancy and extravagance. Gregory, on the other hand, was of a different make. As Leo walked in, she smelled the fresh paint from the renovations. Everything was a little more polished than in the other offices, with a noticeable effort to maintain some semblance of similarity. This was a one-upper-office.

They had transformed the office chairs with the addition of lavish leather, and the recline was so gentle it felt like you were floating. Large windows, but with automated sunshades and not the hideous curtains with grandma flowers. The carpet was thicker, cleaner, and the glass walls facing the hallway were fingerprint free.

And then there was the wall. The brag-wall. Leo had heard about brag walls but had never seen one. The wall was papered with the crisp and proud documents of Gregory's accomplishments. Everything he had done his entire life, except boy scouts and science awards in third grade. There were marathons, triathlons, and other sporting events regularly attended by affluent middle-aged men. He had a black belt in Ju Jitzu and some questionable forms of karate.

Gregory's slow, deliberate clapping echoed through the room as he walked in.

"I see you've already made yourself quite comfortable. In the future, do me the courtesy of waiting for my arrival, so I can grant you a proper welcome. Though, as you may have noticed, my door is always open," Gregory said with an air of arrogance.

"The open door made me think I could just walk in."

"It's not open like that. It's a saying, if you know what I mean." He used his tongue to create a brief, audible click, highlighting his annoyance.

Leo did not know what he meant, but she wasn't going to question it any further. Gregory plopped down at his desk, his shoes thumping against the table.

"So, Leo, tell me what you think about the recent changes I've implemented. I must say, I believe I've outdone myself this time."

This was not the right time to be honest.

"Well. It's different. Different is a word." She scanned the walls nervously.

"Enjoying the décor, Leo? I know it may seem like a bit of a humble brag, but I believe in showcasing my taste and accomplishments."

There was nothing humble about it.

"For example, I enjoy sports. Like running." He gestured at the wall. There were several marathon races. "I don't have all of them on the wall, but those were my favorites. Do you like sports, Leo?" Leo's eyebrows sprung up and away. She wasn't exactly built for athletics. She shook her head, stating the obvious, but kept her eyes on the wall. A screenshot of an error message on a website caught her eye. An 'argument out of range' exception.

"Yes, that one," Gregory chuckled. "It's an inside joke. My Mensa score was so exceptional that it exceeded the range of what they could display. Quite extraordinary, isn't it?" He attempted to convey sarcasm, but the hint of pride in his voice was unmistakable.

She moved closer for a more detailed look. "I wonder what kind of error code they assigned to this one."

Gregory shrugged; his interest seemingly evaporated.

"It doesn't specify which end of the scale it falls outside."

"Are you implying it could be on the lower end?"

"I... I don't know," she stammered.

His gaze bore into hers, his expression anything but amused.

She had to save this. "But clearly you are very intelligent. You are our new CEO, after all."

Stellar effort.

She patted herself on the back.

Crisis averted.

"Anyway, the reason I called you in here for this little meeting is because I believe the two of us need to discuss a minor incident that occurred during the previous meeting."

"Which one? We had seven just yesterday."

Two failed deployments, one missing binary, old certificates, and something about the firewall.

42

"The Fake News meeting."

For one moment, she thought he had seen her folding clothes during the meeting and, consequentially, it was time for flogging, or whatever sort of punishment he preferred. Flogging seemed like his thing, but she couldn't pinpoint *why*. Would she mind? She wasn't sure. Jack and she hadn't explored much. Him being brit and all that comes with it. He was as creative in the bedroom as he was in the kitchen. And if overcooked vegetables and watery coffee could be translated to sex, well, then she'd DHL him back. She didn't finish the thought.

"I believe you overheard parts of a conversation that was supposed to be private, didn't you?" Gregory stared at Leo, his eyes dark and focused, his lips pointy and narrow like a small beak with dinosaur teeth. The meat-eating kind. Leo remained quiet. After all, what could she possibly say?

He continued, "Although nothing has been decided yet, as you've heard, we will have to make some cuts. We have investors that want to see soaring metrics, positive metrics, not expensive ones. So, unfortunately, and it makes me sad to say this, a couple of our offices will have to close. And unfortunately, we won't be able to keep everybody on a remote basis. If I were you, I'd be very clever and not share what you heard. Because I like you, and I trust you, and I can help you maintain a prominent position, with good pay, regardless of the outcome. However, if you find it hard to wait with this information, then I might have to let you go early, and who knows, maybe your team as well. A team with no lead is no team at all, don't you agree?" He attempted to spin the chair, and the sudden shift in momentum made it rock back, stopping halfway around. He grabbed the desk to steady himself and brushed away the hair that had spun into his face.

"It looks like our two minutes are up. Thank you for the lovely conversation," he said in an overly sweet voice. He gestured towards the door, and she took the hint. As she was just about to set off, he offered one last piece of advice.

"Remember, I have eyes and ears everywhere. You will do what is best for us, I'm sure."

Leo nodded, kept her head down, and left.

"What did Gregory want?" Hugo kept up with Leo as she raced down the hallway, amazed he'd arrived in no time. Gerard had probably told him about the meeting.

"Sh!"

"What?" He looked behind them. "His door is closed. He can't hear us. What did he say?"

Leo bit her lip. "Just a pep-talk about the merge."

Hugo let out a long breath and pulled her shoulder to make her stop. "I was worried, you know."

"I know. But I'm sure we'll be fine."

"Okay. Good. Gracias." He slapped her shoulder and skipped to the kitchen.

She hadn't lied. It had been a pep talk of sorts. A tad aggressive, with a sprinkle of threats. But the message had been clear: Roll with it and see where this takes us. We'll take care of you.

8

Ulrik's favorite spot was by the window. It overlooked
the artificial pond that belonged to the in-house behavioral
clinic next door, and sobbing or passive-aggressive fights
occasionally interrupted its peaceful existence. It reminded
him of Spanish soap operas he had been so fond of early
in his marriage when Esther had wanted him next to her
on the couch. True to Swedish culture, the fights and
crying were never of Spanish caliber, he had told Esther
while embracing his fine-cultured prejudice—he had
Spanish friends, after all. It's the subtlety I like, he had
continued, the subtle nuances of the fights, like tones in
red wine. You'd had to be well-versed in familial fights, as
an active participant or educated spectator, to truly
understand and enjoy them. With some salty crackers, fig
jam, and Gruyere. Maybe some grapes. The green kind.
That was back in the day. You had to be vegan now.
Certainly a reason the clinic by the pond was so busy. *The
world is going mental, Esther, but at least I can write books about it.*
Esther had laughed, a burst of pearly laughter like bubbles
in a Prosecco. He wrote a book, many books, enough to
fill a shelf. But Esther's bubbles fizzled out, the wine got

old, and vinegar was all he could make out of their recent conversations.

The window was large and curtain-less, unapologetically bare, and an entry for the light that caught the dust mites sparkling in the air. On the windowsill, with Ulrik's thick fingers stroking it slowly and sensually, a glass sculpture split the rays.

"Ulrik? I think we have another no-show. I couldn't get a hold of Eva, so you might as well prepare for the next one." Marie paused by the door, body leaning in, long pink nails tapping on the doorframe like little daggers. Ulrik couldn't stand the tapping sound she made when she was typing. Gluing pieces of plastic to your fingertips was unfathomable.

"Another?" His voice was barely audible.

"Yes, *another*." Marie tapped the nails on the wood again. A drumroll to match his failings.

Ulrik let out a long breath, dust mites spinning around it, and gave the glass a long phallic stroke. Marie rolled her eyes but quickly smiled when he turned around. "Maybe take a break first, no?"

He returned to his birder position, a brown frame blocking the sun from highlighting the mossy interior. The textile on the chair had gotten so thin and fragile that it might burst into flames if sunlight touched it. Management had suggested they upgrade the furniture, but Ulrik had declined with a huff. It fit his style, he had explained. Management was happy they didn't have to bother with new furniture, and Ulrik was happy he got to keep his fashion statement that he had found in the '60s.

"Thank you, dear," he sighed. "Sorry, thank you, *Maria*." *No dear, honey, et cetera,* he had been warned many times. *It's the vegans, Esther. They ruin everything.* Marie likely subsisted on air and her own reflection. "Who's next?"

"Leo Larsson. At 10. Do you want me to print out the transfer?" *Maybe fax it?*

"No, I can log in."

"Okay. It's the password on the Post-it note. It's a new one."

Marie disappeared, and Ulrik investigated the monitor. It was new. The note was also new. Pink. Marie pink.

Last week, Tuesday, when he had broken in his new orthopedic shoes, he noticed the yellow notes were missing from his monitor. There were none on the floor, nor on the table. They had vanished. The cleaning lady. *Person.* He had tried to log in. *This user or password does not exist.* But Ulrik existed. He was certain of that. Thus, he concluded the password didn't exist. Not in the program, nor his backup- the yellow Post-it note. But why not try the same magic word four more times? Like pushing a button again and again while waiting for the elevator to make it come faster. He knew it was the combined button-push-power that made the elevator hurry. He tried the password again.

After five attempts, it concluded he was senile, or possibly a hacker, and told him to wait for half an hour. Insulted, he called for Maria. *Here. Call this number.* The numbers were barely readable. The pen had fought her plastic daggers and lost. It had merely bled some scribble that took Ulrik three attempts to figure out until a voice introduced themselves as *In- house IT.* Ulrik was surprised by the fluent Swedish and lack of exotic accent.

"My computer has forgotten my password." He panted into the phone. "And the monitor lost my yellow notes. My password. It used to be there." He had pointed at the upper left corner. "Now it's not."

"Okay…" A pause and muffled laughter. "I'll reset your account. Can you bring your computer and ID?"

He had sent Maria.

He sat down, logged in, one key press circling once or twice with his index finger before the press as if it was the first time he had ever seen a keyboard.

Leo Larsson.

Anxiety. Quarter-life crisis.

Quarter-life crisis? Ulrik huffed and powered off the computer. He leaned back and closed his eyes. The sound of Maria's nails tapping against the walls echoed throughout the room, like a woodpecker searching for prey. *Two more hours. I can do this.*

9

Swaying faintly with hands in pockets, Leo watched the frosted glass for shadows. The waiting room was empty, and her breath echoed against the walls. The only thing that confirmed she was in the right place, at the right time, was a piece of paper that had been mailed to her in a handwritten envelope. She moved her gaze from the entrance to the table. Magazines silently giving unsolicited advice. *How to find inner peace. Overcoming anxiety and depression with the help of yoga.* A meditating woman, the non-anxious or depressed type, conveyed the message and judgment with perfect skin and fake eyelashes. Leo glanced left and right and turned the magazine, only to reveal an advertisement for yoga classes. Subsequently, the magazine got to meditate in the bin, and a contented Leo sampled the complimentary coffee.

At exactly 10 AM, the receptionist, the pretty type, gestured for Leo to follow down the hallway, through a door next to her desk, and into a different century.

"Ulrik, Leo is here." Marie tapped twice on the doorframe and disappeared, leaving a trail of sweet, honey-like perfume in her wake. The mossy smell from the walls quickly overpowered it.

Leo watched the door slowly close, ominously. Ulrik remained motionless and transfixed on a monitor.

"This thing is causing a lot of trouble today. Give me a second."

He gave Leo a quick glance and raised his eyebrows. "You look like you'd be good with this kind of stuff."

Leo froze, did a 360, and confirmed there was nobody else there. "Me?"

"Yes, who else?"

She paused, halfway from a cushy seat in a chair draped with green velour that was currently on-trend, but not in that room. The seating was interrupted.

"Why would you think that?" Her eyes darted around the room.

"You are one of those. Technical people."

That was technically correct.

Ulrik sighed. "Young people. You know it all; you know computers. Why can't I log in with my new password?"

She approached him slowly, like a zookeeper with shaky confidence would approach a distressed lion. She had gone without therapy for more than a decade and had forgotten how to act. But tech support was something she could do, albeit reluctantly.

"I can look, I guess."

Ulrik slugged his way towards her, meeting halfway, and reached out a hand for a limp and moist handshake. "Welcome." He eyed her up and down, with no shame or discretion. Leo was there to be judged, after all. That's what therapists do. "I received your journals earlier this week, but I haven't read them. The computer is currently holding them captive. Why they insist on us using that dreadful system, I'll never understand."

An attempt at a smile turned into a grimace, and Leo nodded and pointed at the computer. "How can I help?"

"I can't log in. IT helped me yesterday, but now I can't log in again. I swear they are messing with me." *The old man can't use the computer, ha-ha.* He contorted his face in response to the sound of the imitation laugh, as if it had been genuine.

"It happens to me as well," Leo shrugged, "and I'm not old. It's not only old people that have computer problems."

Ulrik looked at Leo. Did the patient just call him old?

"Sorry. Foot in mouth disease."

"If you are sick, you shouldn't be here."

"Never mind." She nodded towards the computer. "Can I look?"

Ulrik waggled to the side so she could squeeze in next to him. They both stared at the computer for a long, silent second, the login screen gleefully waiting for the next attempt.

Ulrik was the first to interrupt the silence. "Look, I'll try to log in." Fat fingers pressed down the keys, *thud thud.*

"You forgot the *one* and the exclamation mark at the end," Leo interrupted before Ulrik could hit enter. He turned around and glared at her.

"What do you mean?"

"The password, it's missing a *one* and an exclamation mark."

"How do you know my password?"

"It's on the pink note on the monitor."

"Huh," Ulrik rasped. *Esther1!.* "Why does it have a *one* and an exclamation mark?"

"I assume they want you to have a number and a special character?" Pursed lips, terse reply.

"The rest is not special enough?"

She let out a laugh. "I guess not."

Ulrik logged in and stared at Leo's journal. "Esther would disagree but thank you." A small smile escaped through the corner of his mouth.

"You are welcome. It happens to the best of us."

"Let's set this aside for now." Ulrik took a seat and joined. "I'd rather have you introduce yourself. Who is Leo? Let's start there."

"Okay —"

"—And why is Leo here?"

"Do you want me to continue in third person?"

"Is that something you usually do?"

"No, not really. But you referred to me as 'Leo'."

"That's your name, isn't it? Or do you go by a different name?"

"Just Leo."

"Okay let's start over. Why is Leo here?"

Leo nervously shifted in her seat.

"Work has this thing called preventative therapy. At-risk employees have to go. And I had an incident before I moved here that worries them. I told my former CEO. He's a nice guy, talks a lot. And he put in a request for ten sessions."

"Tell me about the incident."

Leo bit her nails and averted her gaze. Dragged her teeth along the cuticle, scraping the thin layer of skin clean off the nail. She'd already scraped clean three nails with inconsistent results. One looked like it had been manicured, the other two like they had been viciously abused.

Ulrik waited patiently, unfazed by the lack of answer. He'd grown accustomed to silence over the years. He drew a square in his notebook and filled it in.

"Fear," he said to break the silence, "is a primitive emotion that is universally observed in the animal kingdom. Humans experience physical changes such as increased heart rate and respiration when they perceive a threat, which is mediated by evolutionarily conserved neural networks. The *fight-or-flight* response to fear can be helpful in some situations, but if it becomes overwhelming, it can interfere with daily life activities or functioning." He drew another square on the paper.

"And it's a raw emotion most of us experience on a daily basis, even though we might not be aware of its presence and effect on our life." He drew a line between the squares. "Do you have fears, Leo?"

She shrugged, her seventh nail busy between her teeth.

"I have many. I'll tell you about one." He put the notebook down. A To-Do list scribbled at the bottom of the page. *Buy cat sand.* Underlined, twice. Leo flashed a smile.

"I've had this clinic for longer than I can remember. Always did well. Until a few years ago. Maybe ten? Patients stopped coming, and we didn't know why. It could be me. Them. The clinic and our old-fashioned ways. And when I sit here with a patient, and silence is our only conversation, it worries me. And the fears tickle the back of my head." He tapped the back of the head. "Here." He straightened up and leaned forward. "I'm not saying this as a form of extortion. I'm just saying that we all have fears."

Leo nodded and took a quick glimpse at the clock hanging behind Ulrik. With only five minutes left, there wasn't any point in sharing anything.

"At its core, fear is always about survival. The clinic surviving, me surviving until retirement. Survival." Leaning back, all his wisdom dried out, he adopted an all-too-familiar posture of an old man.

"I guess my fear is that I'll have another incident. That I'm too mentally fragile to be an adult." No time left. She'd leave it at that. Vague and profound.

"Fear is just that. An emotion. It does not always reflect reality. We are long past our primal state. Fear is a conversation. What do I fear, and why do I fear it?"

Leo reflected on his words, her eyes focused on the window. The light caught the dust, and she watched the particles dance.

Pause. What did she fear? Failure? Rejection?

She leaned back, and the creaking of the chair filled the air. Ulrik was very still. A tiny bit too still. The snoring

53

indicated he was alive, but not very Margaret Thatcher like. His notebook fell onto the floor with a muffled sound, all the secretive writing revealed in a cloud of dust. *Mow the lawn unless the neighbor kid can do it. Tax return?* And squares. A lot of connected squares. Not a single line or drawing about Leo.

"Ulrik? Ulrik!" She nudged him cautiously, like Steve Irwin inspecting a crocodile. "Are you sleeping?"

"No!" He shot up, hit his head on the pendulum lamp, and crashed back into the chair. "I'm sorry, Leo."

"I should go." She got up, yet hesitated. "You can probably just use a card instead of a password. You should check with support." She put on her jacket and opened the door. Marie stood there, her ears aflame, shamefaced for being caught eavesdropping. "And maybe soundproof the walls."

Marie waited for Leo and walked her out.

"Don't worry about him. He is a little odd. He'll see you in a few weeks." She gave Leo a card. Ulrik's face stared back, 20 years younger. "I know. He insists it's still a valid picture. It's practically a water painting with all that pixilation, but it makes his face look smooth as a baby's butt."

"His face does indeed look like a butt," Leo muttered with a smile.

Leo walked out and felt the cold slap of fool's spring, that time of the year when people are convinced spring has arrived only to be bombarded with hail the size of golf balls while wearing a t-shirt and the pants that fit right before fall but now have shrunk. Five minutes to catch the tram. And another five, as it was always late.

On the tram, at the very end of the last car where all the cool kids used to sit, a familiar face stared back at her. Ulrik. Wisely, they pretended they didn't see each other. Ulrik looked out one window, and Leo the other for one awkward hour, until their necks hurt, and the tram screeched at a stop. They honored the transportation solitude, remaining silent and hoping the other one would get off at a different stop. Had it not been for the adjacent nature of their dwellings. Ulrik was her neighbor.

10

"Looks like we have to attend a last-minute meeting."
Leo packed up her laptop and nodded in the door's
direction.

"What now?" Gerard's annoyance was visible on his
face. Gerard, having slept poorly the night before, was
feeling the effects of his restlessness. To make matters
worse, he had pushed a bad script, which only served to
increase his frustration. The API script for updating the
customer API keys was written in Python, a language none
of them took seriously, and there were no tests or
debugging tools installed on either of their machines. He
had used console outputs to trim away all but three
characters from the private API keys, consequently filled
the logs with the private keys, failed to bypass the
retention policy to delete them, and ultimately deleted the
keys during cleanup. In the database. Anna had helped him
parse the log and insert them back into the database. It had
taken all morning, and Hugo had joked Gerard probably
couldn't wait to see sharp again. As in, C#. Gerard had
nearly slapped him, if it hadn't been for the Weaponized
Violence in the Workplace seminar.

"You are two years in and already winning the dad-
jokes award," Gerard had said to Hugo.

"That's my indentation!"

"Intention, Señor."

"I meant indentation," Hugo had replied with a wink.

Not wanting to look up, Leo nervously bit the inside of her lip and stammered, "Something about performance metrics. That's all they said."

"They've already started measuring? That's new to me," Gerard said.

Anna chimed in, her voice soft, "Well, maybe it's a good thing. The metrics can help us improve. Gregory must have something valuable to share with us."

Gerard stared at her as if she were an immortal being, resistant to the traumas of life. "You are something special."

"Thank you!"

"I'll get Hugo."

"Ah, it's great to see you all could make it on such short notice. I trust this doesn't imply that you have too much time on your hands." Gregory laughed, but paused abruptly and scanned their faces. "I'm just kidding!"

"And we are laughing, can't you see? On the inside." Gerard motioned to his face, which was completely devoid of any smile.

Gerard had confided to Leo that he had an extraordinary power. As an OC, Original Coder, he could get away with speaking his mind. A mind that constantly toed the line between what most people would deem acceptable feedback and what was offensive. The longer you stay at the company, he had explained, the more he can get away with. Including speaking your mind. In lieu of a golden Rolex, after fifty years of service, you'd be granted the right to express your opinion. He considered himself to be a straight shooter and an honest guy who simply spoke his mind. Which was code for being rude, according to Hugo.

"Xavier is also joining us." Gregory connected to the screen, and a face pixelated into appearance. Xavier seemed to have a fixed expression with a digit near his nostril, as if he was excavating his nose. Wherever he was, the connection was not doing him any favors.

Gregory began, "We've introduced an array of metrics to evaluate your performance, and one of them is, quite logically, lines of code. You are, after all, software developers, so it's only reasonable to assess whether you're effectively producing software, don't you agree?" He clicked his tongue twice.

The team exchanged glances, unsure who was going to explain to Gregory that software development was more than just adding lines of code.

Gregory went on, "What I've observed, as I'm diligently monitoring your progress, is that our lines of code metric have taken a downturn this week, specifically your code."

"And that's not good, is it?" Xavier added, trying to make himself relevant to the conversation. He was still picking his nose. Gregory rolled his eyes and muted Xavier.

"We refactored parts of the calculations for the price comparison and were able to optimize performance. We've gone down from five minutes to merely three minutes to compare prices from five different providers. That's a massive improvement, and I don't see that reflected anywhere in the metrics." Leo crossed her arms, hiding her sweaty palms under her armpits.

"Our focus in this discussion will be solely on the lines of code metric, and nothing beyond that."

"I wasn't done. And part of that refactoring meant that we could remove a lot of code that wasn't useful anymore. So, we added four lines of code and could remove 300 lines of code."

"Are you saying that you traded 300 lines of code for four?"

"The code was WET, so we made it DRY," Gerard replied with pride in his voice.

"Wet?"

"Sorry, let me explain." Leo wiped her forehead. "WET, as in Write Every Time. Anna attended a People Who Identify as Women Who Code Meetup, where they discussed the DRY principle. Don't Repeat Yourself. Make code reusable; don't copy-paste. She spent the evening refactoring our WET code. It makes the code more *SOLID*."

"Robust?" Xavier reanimated.

"Well, that too. But SOLID, as in, the SOLID principle." Leo relaxed her shoulders. This was going great.

"And when we write SOLID code, we want to KISS," Hugo said.

"DIP helps with that," Anna added. "Also, let's not forget DIE."

"And remove the YAGNI code."

"That was especially important for the REST API."

"To summarize, the code was WET and had a lot of DIE-ying going on. Anna made it DRY and SOLID with a lot of DIP-ping, and removed the YAGNI code, and made sure it was KISS-ing. Makes sense?" Leo flung out her arms.

Gregory's face rapidly turned from a tan beige to a bright red.

"But we need to look over our POCO's. *Un poco*." Hugo laughed nervously as Gregory's face reached a new shade of red.

"STOP IT!" Gregory exhaled, regained his composure, and said in an exaggerated soft voice, "Please stop with the acronyms. No kissing, wetness, dipping, or pocos."

"It does sound like a bad porno." Gerard laughed.

"There are good pornos?" Anna asked in a hushed voice.

Gerard shook his head.

"And now there are fewer lines of code!" Leo grinned.

"But that's horrible! Why would you want to do such a thing? Look." Gregory shared his desktop and zoomed in on a red number. "It's in the negative! RED!"

"Runtime Environment Detection?"

"NO!"

"Network Operations?"

Gregory clenched his teeth, the temporal vein pulsating alarmingly. He glared at the four simpletons in front of him, competing in a moronic acronym-spelling-bee competition that had made him an unwilling participant.

Leo held up her hands in a stop motion. "We can add the code back if that makes you feel better?"

Gregory exhaled. "Yes. That would make me feel better."

"Hugo?" Leo elbowed Hugo, who was holding his laptop in a tight grip. "Want the honors?"

"Not really, boss." His voice was barely audible. As much as he wanted to speak up, he had learned from years of family therapy that sometimes it's better to oblige, however ridiculous, the demand. Do you want to be married, or do you want to be right? He wanted to be married. He wanted to stay employed. He might find himself in a state of bachelorhood if he were to be let go. And with that, Hugo added back the lines of code, committed, and pushed.

"Give it a little and you have your lines back."

They stood in silence, barely breathing, until Gregory gave a subtle nod.

"Outstanding, we've finally achieved a green metric! I fully expect this standard of performance to be sustained. Never doubt for a moment that I'm vigilantly monitoring your progress." With those words, Gregory logged off, and the meeting ended. Xavier reverted to his prior, statuesque demeanor.

The team collected their things and left the room.

"That was quite the spectacle," Leo remarked.

60

"I'm sure Gregory only wants what's best for the company. Maybe we should trust his process," Anna said.

"I guess we should introduce double spacing again," Leo continued.

"And loops, we definitely need more loops," Hugo continued.

"And I can add more comments." Anna shrugged.

Gerard flung his arms out, pure agony on his face. "What are we turning into?"

"Corporate programmers," Leo said, all too knowingly.

"Great. Just great."

Just as they rounded the corner, Gregory caught up with Leo.

"Leo, I'd like your help. Any chance you can come with me?" Gregory gave Leo his most beaming smile, yet the lack of authenticity was as clear as oil in water. Leo stopped abruptly and let the rest of the team continue down the hallway. Hugo turned around, eyebrows raised, but Leo waved him away, sighed, and nodded to Gregory. They shifted their direction and steered to Gregory's office. He tried to chat with Leo, but she responded by increasing the walking speed until they were jogging. By the time they had made it back, they were both bent over, catching their breath. *So much for being a marathon runner*, Leo thought and watched Gregory force his breath to normal. He brushed out invisible wrinkles on his shirt and cleared his voice.

"Leo, dear, I was hoping you could help me move some boxes," Gregory said with deliberate slow enunciation and a soft voice. Leo looked at the boxes in the corner where Elvis's things had been on display on the shelves, in pristine condition. But none of the items were there anymore. They had labeled the boxes with a thick red marker in cursive handwriting: *Elviseses stuff*. Variations of spellings of *Elvis's* were crossed out. She was enticed to point out the grammar, but Gregory was watching her, expecting an enthusiastic yes.

"Unfortunately, I have to get rid of the collection, as I've had more of my things shipped over, and it looks like I'll be staying here for a while."

Leo opened her mouth, but Gregory continued, "So, I'd like to move the boxes to the storage room, and I need your help with that. I enjoyed our last conversation, and I think it will do me good to have some eyes and ears at the office."

With narrow eyes and a red face, Leo held her breath to keep her tongue from saying something she would regret. Gregory grabbed a box and thrust it into Leo's arms, surprising her with the lack of weight she expected from a box full of CDs. The best thing Leo could do right now was to take the box, leave the room and the situation, and maybe locate a pillow she could scream into. She ignored Gregory's parting words and hurried to the storage room, which she opened with the help of her elbow and a push from her hips.

I just must keep it together until the merge is complete, and everything goes back to normal, she thought to herself as she set the box down and leaned against the wall. Whatever the new normal would be in Gregory's world. It seemed less and less probable that Elton would be brought back as the CEO, as it seemed more likely that one of Gregory's minions would seize control with their enthusiastic plans. But with a few more months, the trial employment would turn into permanent employment. Should they, for some peculiar reason, discharge her, she would not be bound to return the relocation fee, and Gregory would certainly intercede for her team and aid them in some form.

She slid down the wall until she sat on the floor with her eyes closed. She stayed perfectly still for the 15 minutes required for the sensor light to deactivate. She had counted the boxes in Gregory's office, and there were six boxes left for her to move to the storage room. It could count as exercise, wouldn't it? Even though the boxes barely weighed more than the paper they were made of.

"All right, let's get this over with," she whispered into the darkness before clapping twice to activate the lights. The lights weren't activated by voice or noise, but Leo liked to pretend that they were. The sharp, stabbing lights hit her eyes, leaving her ironically blind for half a minute. As her eyes adjusted to the sudden light, she saw something written on the box that she had carried. In red, angry marker, *Junkyard*. The boxes weren't being preserved; they were being thrown out. To which Leo deduced they would be next. Gregory would get rid of them in the same manner he had gotten rid of Elton, Elvis's office, and the pristine code.

Unless, of course, Leo intervened - an action she had no intention of taking.

Her solitary show of defiance was to abandon the other boxes in Gregory's office and leave early.

11

Leo opened the front door slowly, grimacing at the crackling sound. She removed her shoes at the door, stepped into the hallway, and held her breath as she closed the door. He hadn't heard her. Slippery like a cracked egg, she slipped into the bedroom with Lion glued to her legs, closed the door, and sat down on the bed. She scrolled through her email.

And *Urgent reply needed*. From that Nigerian prince that needed a loan. Not today my Prince. Not today. She usually had fun with these emails but wasn't in the mood.

She got up. By the window, petting Lion, she scanned the streets. Dirty, wet snow. Lion meowed. A round figure on the street was picking up turds with a pink plastic-clad hand. Tying it together slowly as the wind and rain continued its abuse. A cat on a leash smirked back at the owner. Ulrik? It was Ulrik.

Jack burst in through the door, Lion hissing at his sudden entrance.

"New app idea—"

"—No Jack."

"A dating app for programmers. DateCode. You can input your preferences. Tabs versus spaces, classic, right? Coding languages. Wouldn't have to date a Java developer if you are into Coffee Script—"

She gave him kiss and playfully pushed his shoulder.

"That's a dead language that nobody even graced with a proper funeral—"

He ignored her brilliant remarks. "And more!"

"You don't think there would be a problem with diversity? Maybe, you know, lack of women?"

Jack scratched his chin. "Excellent point. Back to the whiteboard!"

He gave Lion a quick pet, barely avoiding the sharp claws, before retreating to his thinking room. The living room.

Leo turned her attention back to the window. Ulrik lay slouched over the side of a bench, his cat pulling ferociously at the leash. Something didn't seem right. The cat kept pulling, and the tugging moved his hand. The yanking pulled Ulrik down a fraction, but he didn't respond. He was dead. Her therapist was dead on a bench holding a bag of cat shit in one hand and the owner of said shit in the other.

She screamed something about a dead therapist and sprinted down the stairs in her cat slippers.

Running at full speed in her slippers, Leo slid like an Olympian ice-skater across the muddy grass, flailing with her arms in an attempt to regain balance. But as she came closer to investigate, she noticed something odd—his chest was moving ever so slightly up and down. Ulrik wasn't dead at all—he was merely napping. Again. With heavy eyes, he looked up, a frown forming on his forehead.

"Sorry. I thought you were dead."

"Is this a frequent thought?"

"What's your cat's name?"

"Diverting. We can converse about that in session. Margarita."

The name had been chosen by his wife Esther, a fan of the tequila-based cocktail.

"Do you mind if I ask you something?" Leo scratched Margarita's back and avoided eye contact with Ulrik. The amusing conversation about their respective cats' attitudes had dried out. Cats were arrogant, they had agreed, and Margarita had watched them intently as if to warn them not to pursue the conversation further.

Ulrik whistled at Margarita, and she jumped down from the bench. He nodded a blessing.

"Do I have to face my fears? Or is it enough to acknowledge them?"

Ulrik scratched his chin and gave the question a thought. "Sometimes simply acknowledging our fears can be enough to move us forwards."

"However, " he continued, "it depends on what the consequences of your fears might be. What happens if you don't face them? In my case, I've lost many clients, and PP is my last big client. At some point, I'll have to face the consequences of inaction. But today is not the day." His eyes darkened, and he looked into the distance for a minute before breaking the silence again. "However, I do appreciate your technical advice from last session." He smiled and pulled out a keycard from his pocket. A much younger-looking Ulrik stared back. It was the same photo he had on his appointment cards. He looked at the card, the corners of his mouth twitching, and parked the card in his pocket.

"A small step for technology, but a big step for an old man," he said with a fading voice.

This was not the time to tell him that her employer, his last big client, would probably close the office and therefore drop his services. A smile seemed like an appropriate lie.

"I'm sorry about that. Seems unlikely they'll go with a different clinic if they've used yours for a long time." An even better lie.

"It's a family-oriented company," he shrugged, "and that's why they've kept me around."

Leo swallowed and forced a smile. Margarita meowed and jumped back into Ulrick's arms, and he stood up with a groan. Jack had always said groaning when you move your body, unless you are exercising or having sex, meant you were old.

"My apologies, I shouldn't be sharing my personal worries with a patient. After all, you are seeing me so you can work through your worries. I'll see you next week, and we'll have a talk about what keeps you up at night. Maybe that incident of yours?" He pointed at Margarita. "Unless it's a cat that keeps you up."

She walked a few steps alongside them, Margarita keeping her distance. The slippers had gotten wet and soggy, and her arms red from the cold.

"Give Elton my best regards," he said as they parted ways, "and tell him I've sent another CD for his collection. Mr. Music something. Esther won't miss it."

She whispered a thank you and will do, saluted, and jogged home with small, calculated steps to avoid another skating performance.

Performance?

Performance.

Game on, Gregory.

You want performance? I'll give you a performance.

12

The rumors about the Belgian team had spread faster than a fire in a polyester clothing store. It wasn't so much due to acquisition. The rumors were about their impressive and unique project management skills, technical advancement, and superior intellect. They were Belgian after all, as Anna had put it without explaining why. They were said to be gods among the greatest, superstars in the world of software projects.

"And in the email, which I assume you didn't read, Das Lead," Gerard walked ahead of Leo but turned around to look at her, "this team *god* will educate us on the performance metrics. So, we can be performant."

"I'd say we are already performers. A monkey circus," Leo shot back with a wink.

"Gregory doesn't like circuses." Anna caught up with them as they entered the conference room.

"Why would he like fun?" Leo rolled her eyes.

"Not everybody likes the circus. Live and let live." Anna's tone was short.

Gerard connected his computer and swore at the conference docking station until it heard him and connected them. At first, the screen was blank and then a beige blur. The camera struggled to focus, zooming in and out. And there they were. Just two of them. Jan and Luc. Jan's camera was turned off, but Luc's was on. Skin as smooth as a baby's bottom, pouty lips, and piercing blue eyes.

"But he's a child! He can't be more than thirteen." Leo gestured at the conference monitor.

"Excuse me?" the boy on the screen spoke.

"I'm sorry, we are supposed to have a meeting with the Belgian team," Leo replied, red-faced.

"I'm the Belgian team."

"Where is Jan? And the rest of the team?"

"It's just me. I'm the Belgian team. Hello, my new friends." He had a porridge-thick accent, with words that were round and soft, spoken from the back of his palate.

"Is Jan there?"

"I'm Jan," Luc said.

"Aren't you Luc?"

"I'm also Luc."

"Jan-Luc?"

"No, Jan *and* Luc. D'accord?"

Leo and her team sat frozen, mouth agape, confusion draining the oxygen from the air.

Luc sighed with closed eyes.

"I have many roles, oui? I'm the programmer, code-code-code," he tapped his fingers on the keyboard, "and I'm also the product owner, bla-bla-bla." He held a phone against his ear and scratched his chin, pretending to argue with somebody in French. "So I have two names, two identities. And we are the Belgian team. And now we do a big merge with your team!" He presented a generous smile, delighted with his performance. "But we will use our service and merge in yours."

"Why not the other way around?"

"Facile comme bonjour. It is better."

"Good day to you as well," Anna replied. Gerard was having none of that politeness.

"Yeah, really?"

"I've seen the commits. All of them. The code. And commit messages. Forgot file. Forgot file again. No rebase?" He gasped, hand pressed to his chest. "Do you know how that makes me feel?"

"I wouldn't know; it's the first time I've met you. I'm, however, sorry if my commit messages have offended you." The apology was akin to a YouTube apology or a political statement.

"We have more important things to talk about. But can we use the AI-Commit tool for the commit messages? It would make things more, how do you say this, *easy peasy*."

Leo and Gerard exchanged glances.

"AI-generated commit messages are somehow better?" Gerard huffed.

"Consistency. Consistency is key. I've sent you the link."

Leo ran the tool.

"Suggested commit message: A*dded file*."

Gerard turned to face the wall, his shoulders shaking as he tried to contain the laughter.

"We might as well use WhatTheCommit. 'No merge conflict, today was a good day.' At least that one is funny," Leo whispered to an amused Gerard. WhatTheCommit was a website that curated outrageous commit messages from public repositories. It was wildly popular for entertainment purposes.

Gerard rolled his eyes and huffed. A dry raspy sound from a tired man hoping for fewer innovations and an early retirement.

He turned to face Leo and hissed, "I'm not listening to this bullshit."

"Gerard, chill," Leo whispered before returning her attention to Luc. "Let's talk code. Show us the product. We'd love to see what you got."

"Too soon for code. We must talk collaboration first."

"Okay? I mean, the meeting is booked in as Technical Walkthrough. Should we book a different meeting for that?"

"Code collaboration, technical. Jan and I will send the code, easy to read, no need for me. But to work together, we must have good metrics, as per Gregory Handyson."

"We don't even know what the fucking metrics are—" Gerard said before Leo elbowed him. "Please continue, Luc."

"I am Jan now." Luc had switched to the Jan account, which had a different virtual background and a different accent. A fluent American accent, possibly New York.

"I'm just going to go through the performance metrics in random order, although they are weighted differently. Lines of code, lead times—"

"Sorry, but we were waiting for the certificates from the Ops team. We can't provision our own—" Anna tried explaining.

"—number of commits—"

"—we are configuring the calculations in a different service—"

"—new bugs versus solved bugs—"

"—We fix internal bugs every three sprints so—"

"—deploy times—"

"—We were only given one build agent; we can't do anything in parallel! —"

"—And those are the metrics. We must improve those. I sent the full list in the chat." Jan gave a thumbs-up. Anna and Leo watched Gerard, anticipating another volcano erupting.

"Oh well. Ops! Seems like time is up!" Gerard got up with a meek smile, brushed invisible dust off his sleeves, took his laptop under his arm, and left like a disappointed blind-date attendee. At least he left fairly quietly.

Just as they thought he'd left, he returned.

"And this is BULLSHIT. FUCK the metrics." He pulled the door, attempting to slam it, but what started as a

71

good swing of the door slowed down until the doors closed quietly as a whisper.

"I'm so sorry, but I have to join another team meeting for the testing team. But I'll have a look at the board once I'm done," Anna said in an unsteady voice. She avoided eye contact as she collected her colorful pens that she had arranged as a rainbow on the table.

"Sorry about that, Jan." Leo dropped her head.

"Your colleague, the old one, is he always such a contrarian? Or what's the other word, *asshat*?"

"His name is Gerard. And yes, unfortunately, he does have colorful language. And opinions."

"He might be a better fit in a different position then," Jan said without explaining further. "I will ask Gregory. We must work together, and we must do it well."

Leo nodded.

"Do I understand it correctly that all teams will be using the same metrics?"

"That is correct."

"And I assume that the metrics will be used for important decisions further down the road?" She was trying to find a balance between finding answers and not giving away too much. She had never been much of a seamstress, and threading that needle right was harder than she thought it would be.

"Yes, I assume so." His accent slipped, and Luc made a return. He exhaled slowly, finger combed his hair. He gave her a smile.

"Lines of code, bugs fixed vs found, number of commits, test coverage, velocity, lead times, mean times, crash rate, endpoint incidents, and code complexity score. It says they should all have a high score."

"Oui."

"Even code complexity?"

"Especially code complexity."

"Oh."

"I don't see the problem."

"It adds unnecessary difficulty and confusion. It makes maintaining and debugging existing code a nightmare."

"But we can brag?" He grinned.

"I doubt other developers would be impressed."

"But would Gregory be? If we said our code is *very* complex. Here is the score." He held out his hands, palms up.

Leo massaged her temples.

"Well, time is up. Thank you for the meeting, Jan and Luc. Let's swap code links and we'll book a new meeting."

"Merci."

"Mercy?"

"No mercy, *merci*." Luc laughed and ended the call.

No mercy. Not with these metrics.

As Gerard's angry voice spread on the third floor. Leo could sense the seething resentment emanating from him. She located Gerard by his voice. Hidden in a corner room that had *Meditation Room* written on a golden sign. It seemed unlikely that Gerard was meditating, and upon further inspection, the red-faced Hulk was indeed not meditating. Gerard's face was livid - his brows knitted with fury.

"Are you okay?"

"Do I look fucking okay?"

Even on a good day, Gerard didn't appear to be okay. Leo didn't respond.

"Let's get lunch. I know the perfect place."

Gerard was about to say no but remembered he never said no to food. His stomach growled a *yes, please*.

"Looks like your stomach has answered," Leo said with a smile.

13

Leo, being a peach, knew exactly what would cheer Gerard up. With Gerard in tow, she burst through the doors and into the cloud of ammonia and airborne cat hairs. Leo's eyes watered and her throat tightened as she searched the room for anything upright on two legs. Preferably a human. Amidst the mist, a girl with blonde hair waved at her. She squinted, returned the wave, and navigated through the cluster of cats that had gathered at their feet.

"Hi, I'm Sasha!" the girl yelled through the meowing and gestured for them to follow her through a door at the back. The noise and smell subsided as they entered what looked like a miniature cafe. A small area with a window that let in a dusty ray of sunlight.

"What on earth is this?" Gerard stood there with his mouth agape, like a fish out of water.

"It's a cat café!" Leo replied, a wide smile on her lips. She had never brought anybody with her to the café, but Gerard needed this.

Sasha's worried look made Leo continue. "An underground cat café."

"An illegal café, filled with cats?"

"Not illegal. Just…controversial enough for us to keep it a secret. A private club."

Gerard looked around. It looked like the office on deployment day. Absolute chaos.

The walls were lined with shelves filled with animated cat toys, while cats ran around and through the maze of legs and chairs that occupied the center of the room. The air was thick with a mix of energy drinks, sushi, and fur, making it hard to decide where to look first. Everywhere he looked there were cats meowing, climbing on furniture, and jostling for attention.

"Consider yourself an honorary guest." Sasha patted Gerard's arm.

"Right. Right." Gerard pulled out a facemask and snapped the elastic bands into place.

"I'm allergic to cats," he said.

"I'm so sorry! We can go somewhere else."

"I'm joking. I'm hungry. Feed me." He turned to Leo with a displeased expression.

"And here is your table, meowvelous isn't it?" Sasha laughed at her own joke, but the humor was lost on Gerard.

"Let's hope it's not a cat-tastrophe for your allergies."

They placed their orders, and Sasha wrote them down on a notepad shaped like a cat's head. The choice was not a coincidence. Sasha had cat earrings, a knitted cat sweater, a clock with a cat on it, and more cats on the wall than the grand opening of Cats. Sasha was, without a doubt, a cat lady. Cat people were a special breed. Staffed with an unending supply of catnip and tuna, these strange creatures could often be found talking to their feline friends in high-pitched voices or engaged in late-night cuddling sessions.

They watched Sasha walk through the mist of cat hair and dander, bending down to pet each cat that demanded attention.

"Cat obsession has a scientific reason." Gerard looked at Leo, waiting for a reaction. "People who grew up with

75

cats are more likely to have higher levels of a protein called Toxoplasma gondii."

"Protein is good."

"Not this one. It's a protein that has been linked to increased risk-taking behavior, schizophrenia, and even manic episodes."

"Oh."

"Fragile mentally," he added.

"I'd like to think I'm mentally strong." Leo hadn't intended to sound defensive, but her words were short and sharp. She was mentally strong, except for that isolated episode.

"I wasn't talking about you." Gerard gave Sasha a polite smile when she returned with coffee. He rubbed his hands with sanitizer gel, meticulously wiped the cup, and peeled his mask off. The smell of alcohol lingered in the air. "Why are we here?"

"I just wanted to check on you. This place is my escape room. Seemed like a good place to have a calming chat."

"Escape Room is something else."

"It is?"

"Escape Room is a puzzle room concept." He didn't elaborate further, and Leo didn't ask. "I'd like to escape the cat hairs, though." He smiled and rubbed some sanitizer gel under his nose.

By the time they had eaten lunch, Gerard was leaning back in the chair with a furry friend on his lap. Low-allergy kind, Sasha had explained. His coarse fingers were combing the fur, his stomach rising and falling with the cat's purrs.

"I overheard Gregory saying our score was 20% below," Gerard said with a hushed voice as if sharing a shameful secret.

"Below what?"

"Average. Or the worst-performing team. Can't remember. My ears get inflamed when I get angry. Makes

my hearing as bad as a deaf bat. Conductive hearing loss."
He took another sip, careful not to displace the cat.

"We are that bad. Huh."

"Yes. That bad."

They nodded in agreement like two rocking chairs in an old house. Twenty percent. That was truly terrible.

"Hey, guys!" Anna's voice broke the silence. Startled, Gerard leaped up, and the cat on his lap followed suit as though called by its mothership.

"Jesus fucking Christ Anna! You just aged me five years!"

"Sorry!" Anna's face was flushed. She put down the container she had been carrying. "I brought cake!"

"No CAKE!" Sasha's voice was sharp and cutting.

Gerard jumped again, the cat hissing and disappearing into the dimness of cat hair.

"Fuck! You trying to collectively kill me?" He held his palm firmly against his chest, wheezing heavily.

"Absolutely no cake. Absolutely no cake! How are we supposed to make money if we allow guests to bring their own food?"

"This is not food. It's cake." Anna batted her eyelashes and extended the box of perfectly iced cupcakes toward Sasha. "Surely you can let us get away with it, just this time. Pretty please?"

Sasha sighed, but her stern expression softened at the sight of Anna's irresistible smile.

"Well, I guess a few cupcakes won't hurt," she said, snatching the box from Anna, grabbing one, and scurrying away.

"Nobody can say no cakes!" Anna chuckled, taking a seat.

"I'm sure they can," said Gerard. "Gregory would probably not even feed a starving kitten with your cakes."

"Cats aren't supposed to eat cakes," Leo chimed in.

"That's beside the point I'm trying to make here."

"He'd probably give me a low score, though." Anna looked down at the cakes.

"We should make our own scoring system!" Leo grabbed her bag and pulled out her laptop. "Let's see..."

"1. Percentage of days with broken code builds.

None, because we never run the build unless we absolutely must.

2. Number of bugs fixed in a given month.

If we make sure to add bugs more than we fix them, then we'll get a good score.

3. Percentage of time spent on debugging versus developing new features.

We write features while debugging. Debug driven development, DDD, my favorite."

Gerard nodded. It was everybody's favorite programming technique. His eyes dilated.

"I've got a few. Write them down.

4. Code complexity score.

Hugo is an expert at writing overly complex code. Why keep it simple when you can add another crinkle?

5. Average response time for customer inquiries.

Always long. The longer the better. We'll just never reply, right?"

Anna finished her second cupcake, wiped her hands on a napkin, and took over Leo's computer.

"6. Number of outstanding tickets at the end of the sprint.

7. Number of languages used on a project."

"But we only use C#?"

"Languages for the comments! And variables, classes," Anna winked.

"Oh!"

"Two more.

8. Number of times we have to google a solution.

9. Speed at which meetings are attended and completed.

And... number ten is for you, Gerard.

10. Number of times a developer yells at the computer for no particular reason."

"Eight feels like cheating." Leo took the laptop back and turned it around so Gerard could have a read in case his hearing hadn't returned.

"See, that's a much better list," Gerard said after a moment of silence. "A much, much better list."

"We should print it out!" Anna took the laptop again, clicked around, and returned it to Leo. The items had been formatted and the document decorated with flowers and intricate borders. Her cake decoration skills came in handy for document artistry.

They strolled back to the office, finishing off the cupcakes. Gerard looked like he had been crying. Red puffy eyes and blotchy cheeks. They crammed into the printing room.

"Can you make the printer work?" Anna whispered.

"Nope. Never been able to tame that beast. Gerard?"

"I'm not friends with the printer. Ever since that ass-print at the Christmas party, it has refused my presence."

"You did what?" Anna covered her mouth.

"Yes, he did." Leo confirmed. Hugo had told her about it, in detail.

"Hey! Paul!" Gerard waved in Paul, and the room shrank. His smell was strong enough to taste. An avid CrossFit'er that had time for a workout during lunch but no shower. He pressed buttons, pulled and pushed paper in the drawers, but nothing happened.

"Jonathan! Oi!" Paul gestured for Jonathan to get in, and he did, but barely.

"This is cozy. What's the occasion?"

"We can't get the printer to work." Paul gave Jonathan the laptop.

"Are you telling me three developers and an IT support guy can't get the printer to work?"

"Yes!" they replied in unison.

"Shuffle with me." They shuffled until he was closest to the machine. He pulled out the cable and reinserted it. He hit *print*.

"There!"

"You are fucking kidding me. The sales guy fixes the problem." Gerard grabbed the print, and they shuffled out into the fresh air.

"Remind me never to do that again."

"They might put a pineapple on the door if we do."

"A what?"

"Never mind."

Leo, Gerard, and Anna went back to their corner.

"What are we supposed to do with this?" Gerard held up the metrics.

"Put it on the wall," Anna replied with a cheeky smile. Gerard taped it up.

"Funny. Right? Imagine if Gregory were to see this." They laughed. Imagine that.

"Excuse me?" The group turned around. Gregory was standing there with narrow eyes and knitted eyebrows. Gerard hurried and backed against the poster, covering it as best as he could.

"What's behind you?" Gregory enquired.

"Nothing. A wall."

"Really?"

"A plain wall. Not interesting at all." Gerard's voice was shaky.

"As boring as a wall can be. We've submitted a complaint. It's too boring. But it does its job, you know?" Leo smiled tensely.

"I see." Gregory stretched his neck, catching a glimpse of the flowery border.

"Very, very boring," Anna whispered.

"Okay." Gregory gave a nod and turned around. Leo and Anna exhaled loudly. Too loudly.

He spun back.

"And it has nothing to do with these flyers?" He held out a thick stack of papers. Hundreds of copies of their fun metrics. All the print attempts had arrived simultaneously.

"It's just a suggestion," Leo replied and tried to grab the papers.

"And you were planning on handing them out?"

Gregory thrust the papers into Leo's arms. "Stop fucking around, alright?"

"Yes sir."

"Do you want a cupcake?" Anna presented the cake box.

"A…what?"

"Cupcake…" she whispered so quietly that only dogs could make out her reply.

Gregory looked around. Brushed the wrinkles out of his shirt. He grabbed a cupcake and took a bite. "These are fantastic!" He ate the rest of the cupcake in two bites and licked his fingers.

"Focus on the merge, okay?" He sped off.

"I think we just lowered our score." Leo sighed. "Unless that last cupcake had drugs in it. But I don't think they do. My toothache is back." She rubbed her chin and threw the papers in the bin.

"I like our metrics more than his," Gerard said with a downturned smile.

"Me too," Anna added.

14

Dressed in confidence, polished shoes, and dressy jeans, Jack guided Leo through the alleyway. A man too old to be a bouncer yet dressed as a bulldog in a suit waved them in. Leo deduced that it was a club from the entrance layout. The walls were adorned with posters of people with contorted faces, bent over as if in pain, spotlights catching the spills on the old tables.

"Is this a BDSM sort of thing? You know I take pride in my prudence. If I want torture, I'll just look at Hugo's code. No spanking needed," Leo said dryly and linked her arm with his. "You smell nice today."

"No, no, it's a standup club. Those are people laughing."

"So that's what laughing looks like. I'll add that to my memory bank. I might be able to replicate that when you tell a joke."

"There will be plenty of opportunities in the next hour." A mischievous smile on his face.

"I was afraid so."

Jack squeezed her hand. "Are you sure you are up for it? With the toothache and all?"

"Yes. It will pass."

"Why won't you see Dr. Fazim again?"

Why? It had been a visit that had left her in tears. Within ten minutes, the dentist had told her the teeth would rot away before she turned forty, and that she'd had to stop eating fruit and vegetables, commit to OMAD, one meal per day, and brush her teeth four times per day with prescription toothpaste. The only thing she could commit to was the brushing, in theory, anyway.

"Because he isn't Martin."

Martin. The Peterborough dentist she had left when they had moved to Sweden. They had had a peculiar relationship, with Martin having an unusual interest in her dentures and the width of her smile (or lack thereof).

"I don't want you to see Martin. The thought of somebody obsessing over your teeth to the point of emailing you in the middle of the night from a private email address to share photos he took of your teeth is bonkers."

"Martin forever." She made a heart shape with her fingers and laughed. "I like to think we had something special."

"You and me, or you and Martin."

Leo shrugged. "Both?"

Jack pinched her side. "Watch it, young lady!"

"Come on," Jack pulled out a chair for her, "it's going to be fun!"

"Isn't it ironic that we are sitting at a standup club?"

Jack laughed. "It really is. But you do standup at work sitting down, right?"

"I hope the tickets weren't expensive." She bit her lower lip.

"We can afford it," Jack said and kissed her forehead.

If only you knew, she thought, but quickly pushed the cloudy thoughts aside. They'd be fine. They were always fine.

They ordered some beers of unknown brand and origin but with the right alcohol content to get the date started.

Prior to the move, they had agreed on a weekly date night, and that they'd alternate who plans the date. Leo stuck to the movie and popcorn dates, while Jack was set on exploring the city and its variety of entertainment. It was far from the same as in London, which makes sense considering that Gothenburg only had half a million inhabitants compared to London's nine million. Nonetheless, there were always some charming local events that could give them a break from the mundane everyday life during the terrorizing winter and its never-ending darkness. Leo scanned the room that would be her prison cell for the next hour. She'd usually muster more enthusiasm on Jack's dates, but she had spent what little energy she had at work, and despite begging Jack to reschedule, he had insisted they go.

To maximize the experience, Jack had made sure they sat close enough to the stage to catch the droplets of saliva from the amateur humor artist. The stage was merely a section marked out with duct tape and harsh spotlights. A lone microphone hung with its head, waiting for clammy fingers and dry lips.

"Ladies and gentlemen! Are you ready for Sarcasm King?"

"If he hadn't said king, I'd think it was you," Jack laughed.

"If I wanted sarcasm, I'd just give Gerard a call."

Jack drowned his beer and gestured for another. He was going to need a few more beers to get through this or through to Leo. The curtains were pulled to the side, and the Sarcasm King made his entrance, bowing to avoid the hanging lights. As he stretched to his full length, the top of his head disappeared behind the spotlights, his hair brushing the ceiling.

"He is from the Netherlands," Jack explained. The King walked back and forth on the stage, cocky as a rooster strutting around the barnyard. An accountant by day, he had been told he had a flair for show biz and a unique sense of humor. With the risk of being one of the contestants shown during halftime of a televised song contest, the ones that insist their mother loves their voice, he had signed up for the comedy special. What's the worst that can happen? If they don't laugh, then he'd laugh. And that's what he did. Nervously looking for a clearing between the lights, he giggled uncontrollably like a serial killer at a teenager disco. He grabbed the microphone, swinging it by its tail. The feedback echoed in the room, and the crowd moaned at the auditory abuse. "Don't admit defeat," he whispered to himself and doubled down on the swing. Another high pitch sound tore through the speakers.

"God damn it," Leo grunted and covered her ears.

"Awww! I haven't even started, and you are canceling my voice?" The Sarcasm King, also known as Peter Karlsson, cocked his head, his chin barely visible under the lights. Leo leaned back and hid in the shadows with an exasperated sigh. Jack looked at Leo with a stern, unwelcoming expression. His eyes were cold and unyielding, conveying his displeasure in the situation.

"Are you sick, Jack?"

"No! I'm trying to give you a disapproving glance!"

"You looked sick doing it." Leo shrugged. And a lightbulb moment later, "Why are you disapprovant?"

"That's not a word."

"It is now. I just made it a word."

"You can't—"

"—there. Added it to Urban Dictionary. It's now a word."

"I don't know what's going on with you, Leo, but you've been gloomy and depressive. More than usual."

Peter had started his second act and picked up some confidence along the way. With his face hidden, he had to work harder with his body, miming as best as he could with his hands. The self-deprecating jokes were popular among the audience, but unfortunately all too true for him.

Merely describing his life, which consisted of crunching numbers, arguing with his wife, and surviving on little sleep and a bullfrog toddler that defied the laws of sleep.

"Ladies, amirite? They break your heart but won't let you die, so you get a frikking break! Amirite?" Peter finger-gunned Leo.

"When's *your* break?" Leo shot back, and the audience roared. Peter cocked his head to get a better view of his opponent, but Leo pushed her chair back and hid in the shadow. Jack apologized to the comedian, but Peter had moved on to another table at the front.

"Look, Jack, things aren't okay at work. You know this. I've got a lot on my mind."

"Can't you pause your mind and spend some time with me instead?"

"Easy for you to say. It's not like your mind is under a mountain of stress; you can relax and take it easy."

"Would it make you feel better if I were?"

Probably, yes, Leo thought.

"No, of course not. Look, I'm sorry. I'm really stressed about the work situation. If we don't do better, I'll be without a job. We'll be without a job." Leo prayed he wouldn't do the *I work as a bitcoin investor monologue*. She had seen how the stocks had been doing. The stocks were crashing like a house of cards in a hurricane, but Jack kept buying cards and building, ignoring the stack of ruins. He had never been a good gambler; he simply didn't know when to call it quits.

"Leo, I'm a bitc—"

"There's my haggler!" Peter was ready for act three, and he needed help. "What do you do for a living, my lady?"

"She's a software developer," Jack exclaimed with pride in his voice.

"A lady programmer? What a rarity! And what do you do, programmer lady?"

Jack elbowed Leo and mouthed, "Please?"

"I'm in charge of the kilobytes."

Peter bent down and looked at her with a confused expression.

"But tell me, lady—"

"Just call me Leonarda."

"But tell me, Lady Leonarda, do you ever go to the beach?"

Leo's pale skin answered for her, but Peter was going for something else.

"…to get a byte of sunshine?"

"You can tell she has never gotten any bytes of sun. Probably lived in a basement, at home, pissing in a bottle!" a male voice from the depth of the crowd reverberated across the room.

"What a delightful stereotype. Tell me, lady, are the bottles safe with you?"

"Not if they are in close proximity to that guy's head."

The crowd gasped and laughed.

"And tell me, lady, do you code like a girl?"

"Do you write your jokes in comic sans? Cause they seem as dated as the font."

Peter jumped back as the crowd roared with laughter again.

"I do," he whispered, chin down and face red. "It's a timeless classic. Fun and whimsical." He drank some water and returned to the other table where an excited young man and his date were waiting for the next insult.

"Leo, I'm just worried you'll end up in the exact same place as you did before we moved here. Working long hours, taking work home with you, and feeling constantly exhausted. That's you right now, isn't it?"

Leo shrugged.

"But it's temporary, Jack. Things will go back to normal soon."

"You are going to burn yourself out if you keep doing this. You are constantly 'on the clock'. At least mentally. And while I can handle your irritability, and maybe the standup comedian can as well, I doubt your colleagues will appreciate it."

"I'm only irritated when I'm at home. I can keep my shit together at work."

"Well, lucky me then." Jack smiled and placed a hand on her arm. His hands were always warm. Hers always cold. Ironic, considering she spent more time exercising her fingers on the keyboard than he did.

"I'm just saying that it's important to take time for yourself and practice self-care."

"I know."

"Can you at least talk to your therapist about it?"

"Sure."

"Does he know about your breakdown?"

"I've mentioned it."

"All of it?"

"Even the Godzilla incident?"

"I might have left that out."

"Destroying office equipment for the cost of half a million dollars was a costly affair, mentally and financially. It's worthy of a mention."

"They exaggerated the value. The monitors were older than an episode of *Friends*. Rachel was still bra-less when they bought them, the refresh rate of a snail."

"Talk to him."

"About the awful work lights. At least I got a tan for the first time in my life. And probably skin cancer."

"Talk to him."

"I should have sued them for pain and suffering."

"Talk to him."

They watched Peter do an impromptu song-and-dance to honor his life as an accountant.

With questionable rhythm and style, the comedian wiggled his way between lyrics and dance moves that painted a funny picture of his days crunching numbers. A mix of admiration and hilarity ran through the crowd as they watched him jive and jiggle in the tiny space on the stage until he hit his head in the spotlights and busted his eyebrow.

"Is that blood?" He looked at his cupped hand and the dark red liquid pooling in the folds. "Funny thing, did you know I have something called vasovagal syncope—"

He nosedived before he could finish his sentence.

"I guess that's the end of the show. Let's go grab some food," Leo said and stood up. "The vampires will take care of him."

15

The relentless darkness during the winter months had hit Leo hard. The darkness was like a mischievous monkey that stole all her smiles and replaced them with frowns, she thought. If she had been a smiley person to begin with. And she wasn't. She turned to lie on her back, the stack of pillows collapsing from the motion. Jack was already up, immune to the dark mode they lived in. He was living his best day yet, humming away on a commercial he had seen on TV. She pulled the blanket to her chin and waited for the blue light from the therapy lamp. At 07:30 the alarm would ring twice, and the intense light would fill the room, and she'd meditate for ten minutes. As soon as the light turned on, and the room turned into an aquarium, Jack rolled closer to her.

"True Messaging."

"What?" Leo couldn't hide the annoyance in her voice.

"A messaging app that analyzes your facial expression with the help of AI and lets the other person know how you truly feel. Live. IRL. While messaging."

"That's disturbing on so many levels, I don't even know where to start."

They looked at the ceiling. Bright blue.

Leo continued.

"So that's a no from me."

Jack spun his thumbs.

"Mmm. Okay. I'll come up with something better. But it must be something with AI. That's what people want. And sometimes you just must give in to demands."

"Mmm."

"Such as performance metrics."

"I'm not a performer."

"I wasn't talking about you. Just, in theory."

Jack kissed her on the forehead, threw the covers to the side, and jumped out naked as a newborn. His footsteps subsided, and Leo returned to her light therapy.

By the time she realized that the therapy lamp had malfunctioned and failed to turn itself off, she was already late. With the heavy snow layered with ice, she'd have no chance to bike to the office.

"Bye!" Jack didn't respond. He was busy milking the last drop out of the warm water. Leo slammed the door behind her and ran down the steps two at a time. She made it to the tram stop with less than a minute to spare and without her laptop bag and wallet. The tram slowly pulled away from the stop and started its journey. The poles holding up the electrified wires slowly creaked and moved in time with the rhythm of the cabins.

She watched the stadium glide by, hockey fans gathered on the street. Battle gear, purple and green, ready to defend their heroes as long as they had beer, and it was before dinner time. The tram was slowly filling up again, and Leo did her best to fill in the seat so she wouldn't be the first choice for a seat companion when all the double seats had one occupant. Being skinny, and quiet, made her an excellent candidate. Scrolling through the internet and battery life, she didn't notice the white baseball caps until it was too late. Leo's face went paler than a ghost in a snowstorm. A blue jacket and white baseball cap flashed between the crowd. They were there. On the tram. Ticket controllers.

"Tickets, please!"

She had no tickets. Darn it. She got up, stumbled for half a step, and jumped out the open doors just as the doors closed and the tram started rolling. The knees kissed the ground, a violent teenage kiss with no direction or experience.

"Are you all right?"

"Yes." Leo stood up, rubbing her knees, a victorious smile. *Like a pro!* This was also why she never did skateboard or inline skating when she was a kid. Not that her parents would have let her do such unsophisticated sports.

"Looked like a rough landing, but glad you are okay! Can I see your ticket please?"

Leo looked up, the sun hiding the face wearing the white baseball cap. No other clue needed. Just the hat.

"I don't have one," she said, trying to walk away but being gently pulled back by an arm in a blue sleeve.

"Let's go get you a ticket then, okay?"

"I can buy one!" She tried to wrestle away, but it was no use. The blue sleeve had a firm grip, and she had spaghetti for arms.

"I don't think so," said the voice behind the baseball cap. "You see, you've been riding without a ticket for the past few stops."

"I'm a tourist, I don't speak Swedish. Or English."

"You are speaking it now—"

Fair point.

"—and we met this morning. Remember?"

Leo shaded her eyes, and an unshaven face got its contours. A decent jawline and big white teeth. A little bit too big. A lanyard strangled an ID card. The same face stared back, with the exact same expression. *Jim.*

"Yes, it's Jim from last week's episode of *I no speak Swedish.*"

Pride blossomed in her chest. It had been fantastic acting on her part. She grinned widely with her much smaller pearls. "It worked last time!"

"It was my first time."

"Wow! Sames! Look at us two, non-virgins and all. Joke aside, I'll buy a ticket. Just let me go!"

"Nope, sorry. You'll have to come with me to the office."

"The office? What is this, the 1950s?"

"If you'd like to make a complaint, you can do so at the office. And the office is from the 1950s."

"You got to catch me first!"

And with that, Leo took off running. It was her only chance. If she could make it to the other side of the street, she could lose him in the crowd.

"Hey! Come back here!"

She could hear his footsteps behind her, but she didn't dare look back. Her eyes were glued to the ground. Her body had forgotten how running worked. It was all a jumble of arms and legs, like a ragdoll being dragged by a dog.

"GO IFK!!!" she yelled through the crowd, zig-zagging through the beer-fueled fun. A hand grazed her arm, but she ducked and weaved like a champ.

"IFK is fucking football! Football sucks! Football SUCKS!" The crowd booed.

"I meant," she quickly read the closest purple shirt, "GO Frolunda Indians!"

The crowd cheered.

"It's not Indians anymore, HC! Frolunda Hockey Club!" A shaky voice barely escaped the crowd.

"FUCK THAT SHITE! FROLUNDA INDIANS FOR LIFE!" the dark voice roared, and the crowd cheered again.

She was so close! If she could just make it to the other side-

"Oof!"

A body collided with her and sent her flying. The world turned upside down, and then she hit the ground as the purple dancing mess went vertical and then faded out. She woke up on a cold staircase, wearing a Frolunda foam hand. A security camera stared down at her. Someone somewhere was being entertained. Leo exhaled. Jim was nowhere to be seen. She climbed up the last stairs and leaned against a frosted door.

The door opened, and a cat stared at her. How did the cat open the door? Was the cat real? *Great. I have a concussion.* The meeting with Gregory had started five minutes ago. Maybe they'd close the office before she even got there.

"Leo? Are you in good health?" Ulrik towered above her, the imaginary cat in his arms.

Leo was at a loss for words, gaping. So, she did the only thing that was sensible. She screamed.

"Oh dear!" Ulrik jumped back and squeezed the cat.

"What's going on out there?" Marie's voice seeped out through the open door.

Leo would never dream or hallucinate about Marie. This was not imaginary.

"I'm sorry. When I have a bad dream, that tends to help. Screaming."

"The scream brings you back to consciousness?"

"No, but it wakes up Jack, and he brings me back."

Ulrik snorted. Margarita looked down at Leo with narrow eyes.

"Might I enquire as to why you are taking a seat outside my office?"

"It's a long story. I've got to go." Leo stood up and brushed her clothes. A stream of blood ran down her leg from her right knee, where a small stone was lodged into her exposed skin.

"Should I request that Marie provide you with something for your injured knee?"

"Probably a good idea."

94

"Mar—" Ulrik didn't get to finish his sentence.

"—I'm onto it!" Ulrik put the cat down, and she scurried away.

"Bring-your-cat-to-work-day?"

"Just today. My beloved Margarita has an appointment with the vet. I am worried that she may be feeling a bit depressed. With Esther being gone."

Leo finger combed Margarita's fur, and the cat purred with delight.

"Oh. I'm so sorry."

Ulrik accepted the MedKit from Marie and handed it to Leo so she could patch up her knee. The stone that had wedged itself into her knee plopped out with a small bounce down the stairs.

"How is your work faring these days? Is everything going satisfactorily with regard to your professional endeavors?"

Leo stared at him.

"How is work?" Marie yelled her transcription.

"Horrible. I've tried to gently guide the team in the right direction. To do better. Perform better. But Gerard just says pretty is what works. And soon we'll have no work. And that's not pretty. Stupid metrics. Did I mention we are the worst? The worst team? I can't make everybody change how they are overnight. Let alone me." Leo inhaled deeply. "Sorry for rambling."

"That's an unfortunate situation," Ulrik replied and glanced at his clock. He had replaced his old watch with a digital watch, and the digits were abnormally large.

"I'll leave. We have an appointment on Thursday?"

Ulrik turned around, waiting for Marie.

"Yes! 9AM."

Leo looked at his clock. The meeting would have finished by the time she got to the office.

"Is that a smartwatch?" Leo asked.

"It would depend on how you measure intelligence. I appreciate the simplicity of this digital watch. It does not attempt to measure my breaths or track my whereabouts or monitor my digestion; it just looks like an intelligent device Makes *me* look smart." He smiled. "Maybe even *on-fleek*."

Looks like. Just looks like. Leo repeated the words in her head. What if the team just looked like they performed well? If the pipeline made it look like they did the right things at the right time.

"THANK YOU!" Leo shouted louder than she had intended, the excitement from her absolutely ridiculous plan bursting through her vocal cords. She grabbed Ulrik's hand, shook it violently, and ran down the stairs until her knee reminded her of its state and left her crumbled at the corner of the staircase where the dust bunnies had gathered for their monthly meeting. She waved with a shaky smile, pushed to her knees, and slowly walked out with a telling limp.

16

Leo stood at the tram stop, a triumphant look on her face.

Despite all odds being against her, she would be able to save the office from closing. Her mind was racing with a sense of satisfaction.

It was the best idea she ever had - and an impressive feat, considering the number of questionable ideas Leo had landed on through the years. She got on the tram.

This was the best bet she had on improving the team's performance metrics. She pulled up her calendar. In a whisper, in the janitor's closet where they were standing too close, her informant revealed that Friday was the metrics day. Friday at six PM. After the weekly deploy. Which, for reasons unbeknownst to her, always was scheduled to be on the last working day and last working hour of the week. The information came from a very talkative Elton, AKA the informant, who happily shared internal information in exchange for the opportunity to share fun facts and anecdotes about his life.

She stared at the calendar. She had no idea what day of the week it was. Monday. It was Monday. She had less than a week to pull this off. It would be like trying to paint the Mona Leo with a cotton swab. Her smile tensed as she remembered all the hard work and long hours that had gone into making this happen. Risky. But she'd pull through.

The tram rolled in like a sleepy giant, shaking and creaking as it came to an abrupt halt.

Leo covered her ears. The city of Gothenburg in Sweden notoriously invested millions in a fleet of trams from Italy that were designed for warm climates and quickly proved to be ill-equipped for the cold Swedish winter. As soon as snow fell, these trams became virtually unusable and could not handle the conditions at all. Needless to say, this was an incredibly expensive mistake by the city's officials that has become a running joke among locals. To make matters worse, the city was unable to get a refund from their Italian suppliers - what was supposed to be a reliable form of public transportation quickly became an object of ridicule. The joke around town is that, "If you're looking for reliable transportation in Gothenburg, just don't buy tram tickets—buy tickets for Italy instead!"

Leo climbed onboard and looked at the clock on the glitchy display at the entrance. Half a workday left. She couldn't afford to waste more time.

"Tickets, please!"

Leo had never been to Italy, and her current financial situation didn't leave much room or money for spontaneous trips to Italy. So instead, she just didn't buy any tickets at all. Not for Italy, nor for the tram. If the trams were missing in action fifty percent of the time, she'd only get tickets every second month. The controllers didn't agree with her strategy.

As soon as the doors opened, she jumped out. The next tram was in half an hour. Even less time.

Damn it. She opened the tram app, bought a ticket, and pushed through the closing doors.

"You again."

"Yes, I'm sorry. I have a ticket now," Leo replied meekly and presented her phone like a gift.

He grunted and scanned the ticket.

"Don't make it a habit."

"Buying tickets?" Leo grinned. He shook his head, a stern look on his face.

"That's not funny."

He scanned the next passenger, and Leo went back to planning. The tram screeched again. She thought about *The Duckie Incident*. A screeching sound had escaped the receptionist's mouth when Leo swung the keyboard the second time. Leo had growled like a lion, she had been told. Lion the cat would have liked that, but then again, he was psychotic, a common feline trait, and he would have done the same if born with a mutation that gave him opposable thumbs.

Maintainers burnout.

That's what they had called it. Although they had used a more colorful language for the big incident. Her old doctor, and Jack, seemed to have conspired against her. Cautioning her about the possibility of working overtime. And it honestly wouldn't be a problem if the day had more hours. It would also help if she was better at planning. And not losing her trail of thought. At least staying on the trail a bit longer before wandering off. And better focus. That would have been beneficial. She looked out the window. She'd manage her time and attention better this time.

The Lipstick rolled by. An iconic architectural landmark. With twenty-two levels tapering at the end and the last five painted bright red, it looked like lipstick. Or a penis with a UTI.

No way… She sighed loudly and pressed the stop button long and hard. She had missed her stop. The tram continued. The next stop would be in the Old Town. Another half an hour delay.

She disembarked from the tram. Her euphoric feeling after the grand idea was giving way to annoyance. At least she had a tram ticket and could grab the first tram back.

She scanned the departure screen. Canceled. All departures were canceled. Her delay would be prolonged. This was worse than being late for your own wedding. She made a mental note not to rely on public transportation if she were to wed.

Leo's cheeks flushed, and her heart rate quickened as anger began to bubble up inside her. She had managed to time her arrival at the wrong tram stop to be rewarded with more delays. With a few choice words for the transit system, she started running, determined to make it in time despite the setback.

Although her lack of past athletic endeavors, she knew she had gotten a fraction of cardio workout from the biking she had done throughout the years. If push came to shove, she could run for at least a kilometer or two. If only she hadn't injured her knee earlier. Mid-leap, her knee reminded her of the mishap — a sharp pain that brought an agonizing wince to her face.

The knee made a grinding sound, like sandpaper rubbing against metal. The pain was worse than having to listen to a ten-minute lecture from Jack about why it was so important that she didn't push herself too much. With the image of her boyfriend nagging her in her mind, she switched her limping run into a rapid penguin walk and cursed all the way to work. She'd had to tell Jack that he had inspired her through the grueling journey. If she ever made it back home.

"Are you okay, Leo?" The receptionist stood by the entrance desk, a look of surprise on her face.

Leo smiled with her lips pressed into a tight line, trying to shake off the fatigue and despair that seemed to cling to her like an invisible weight.

She managed one step then another until she finally made it to the elevator and up to the team office. With shaky fingers, she opened it—relief washing over her. They were all still there.

"You are mighty late," Gerard groaned from his corner.

"But I've saved you two cookies!" Anna gave Leo a green, sparkly box. *Some carbs would do me good*, Leo thought, and gently pulled out a delicate cookie wrapped in rice paper.

"LEO!" Hugo's enthusiastic calling made Leo choke on the cookie, her dry mouth, unable to maneuver the pieces.

"Why are you in? Don't you have the flu?"

"I'm better." Hugo pointed at his mask. "Besides, this helps. I don't want to let the team down, you know?"

"He is scared of Gregory," Gerard explained. Hugo looked down. He was afraid of Gregory.

"Whiteboard, now." Leo gestured for them to follow her to the whiteboard.

"Did your kids draw on it?" The lower half of the board had what looked like a drawing of a house and a tree.

"No, it was me." Hugo squinted, smile-lines framing his eyes.

"I'm sorry."

"Don't be!"

Leo was. Sorry about his lack of drawing skills. It would have been nice to have somebody on the team that could draw. Unless Anna had some mad skills, they'd be out of luck if they had to create manual mocks or win a game of Pictionary.

"I have given the metrics a lot of thought, and honestly, we got to ace this. We can't be at the bottom, guys."

"Bottom guy?" Hugo's eyes grew.

"*At the bottom.*"

Gerard huffed and looked out the window. Standing by the window, his body had the same shape as Ulrik's. It had never occurred to Leo that the two had some common traits. Silhouette. Grumpy mood. Longing for retirement. "I don't see how we can suddenly become a top-performing team. We are laid back. We are Swedes. It's in our blood to take it slow." Gerard was French, Hugo Mexican, and Anna from Greece. It was beside the point, though, Gerard insisted when Leo questioned his phrasing.

"Can you give me a few minutes?"

"Five. I can give you five."

"Just five?"

"It's five to four. And we finish at five."

"Wouldn't that leave an hour?"

Gerard laughed. "Everybody knows that four to five is just pretend."

It was true. Only sales were still around after four.

"Where are the whiteboard pens?"

"Fredrik probably has them," Gerard replied, his voice still raspy and annoyed.

"Why?"

"He's an *agile coach*. He is addicted to that stuff. Whiteboard markers and Post-it notes. That's his whole career, right there. And the fucking-colored dots."

Anna giggled. Fredrik did have a thing for the pens, papers, and dots. If they were to invade his privacy and go through his backpack, they'd probably uncover a nice stash of stolen pens.

Triumphant Leo held up a pen.

"I found one. Now close the door. This is top secret. Not even Tim is invited."

Anna closed the door.

Leo wrote down their score: twenty-eight. And the next Belgian's score, hundred-and-nine. Nice work, Luc. And Jan. She circled twenty-eight twice. She drew a large square for each metric and a few keywords for how they'd increase the score in the span of four days. Fuck. Three days. Short days. Gerard days.

"These are the metrics we *can* change. In our own way. We are going to," she wrote with large thick letters, "GAME THE METRICS/SYSTEM."

"Sounds evil. I like it." Gerard moved closer, his breath audible and excited, like a teenager on a first date.

"Okay, listen up. This is what we are going to do…" Leo uncorked the pen and started writing on the board.

17

Tim and Elton were like two peas in a pod. They'd known each other for as long as Tim had been employed there, four years and three weeks. When Elton had been a CEO, they would have a standing meeting every Monday at the end of the day to go over numbers. There were no numbers, of course. It had only been an excuse to wrap up the saddest day of the week on a good note and with a glass of wine in Elton's office. When Elton stepped down and Gregory up, they'd kept the rendezvous and upped the wine as the new situation at work required higher alcohol levels. That particular Monday they had tried their best to avoid talking about work, but Gregory had left the recent performance numbers in the form of large, gory diagrams on Elton's desk.

"I don't even know why he dropped them off at your desk," Tim had said.

"I guess he wants *to tell everybody...*" Elton had hummed the rest of the lyrics. Although, he shamefully thought, *The Bitch Is Back* would have been a better song.

"I know you worry, Elton, but it's a great team. Have faith in them."

They had walked together down the hallway, one small pea and one big pea, discreetly disposing the plastic cups they had used for the wine.

"Look," Tim had said and pointed at the team room, which let out a bright light through the ajar door, "half-past five, and they are still hard at work!"

The door opened before Leo had a chance to reflect on her lack of coverup in case somebody uninvited walked through the doors. Nobody visits a software development team without a notification or enquiry (which would most likely be denied). However, the shock was bigger for Tim.

Standing in the doorway, he watched the chaotic scene starring four frantic developers trying to wipe out a whiteboard.

"Wipe it!" Hugo shrieked.

"I'm trying, but it's a permanent marker! Who the hell leaves a permanent marker next to a whiteboard?"

"Fredrik." Anna's voice was barely audible in the commotion.

"Quick! Cover!" The quad huddled in front of the whiteboard, Anna extending a cake box above her head in an attempt to cover the whiteboard.

"What the h—" Tim interrupted himself and turned to face a curious Elton.

"Is there something fun going on?"

"Yes…secret! It's a secret planning for…a secret person."

Elton winked. "Oh…a secret surprise for somebody…"

"Yes! Yes! So, unfortunately, you have to leave. Now." Tim pushed Elton away from the door. Elton giggled and left with a cheeky smile.

"What's going on? This looks highly litigious."

"He covered for us. He is in!" Hugo slapped his hands together into a wet, nervous clap.

"Is that Gregory? With a CD wedged in the head?" Tim stared at the drawing, thick black lines outlining a plan, and drawings of a tall man with a CD wedged into his head.

"You will be on my Pictionary team!" Leo clapped Tim on the shoulder as he walked in.

"Pictionary?"

"Thanks for having our back, boss," Hugo said sheepishly and bowed.

"Why is Hugo wearing a face mask?"

"The flu, boss."

"The flu?"

Gerard stepped to the side, exposing the last bit of the whiteboard that they had covered with their frail bodies. Tim forgot about the flu.

The whiteboard outlined the plan.

Lines of code: Add at least one comment for every line.

Bugs fixed vs found: Don't report new bugs. Fix all easy bugs even if low gain.

Nr of commits: Split everything into small commits. Max one file per commit. Use AICommit to generate messages. Change file names and add whitespace.

Lead times: Create easy tickets and rush them out. Skip QA and staging.

Code complexity: Add nested conditions, combine methods, use as many variables as possible, lots of inheritance, and add even more variables for good measure.

'We love Halstead Volume' was enclosed by a heart.

"What's Halstead Volume?"

"A measure of the number of tears a programmer sheds while trying to understand the code," Gerard explained.

"It's a complexity score. It measures the size of an algorithm based on operators and operands. That's the ELI5 answer."

"ELI5?"

"Explain it like I'm five."

"The level we should use with Gregory. He can't be much older than that," Gerard hissed.

"Ageism is not a good look on you, not this close to retirement anyway," Leo retorted.

"And we want more code complexity? Last time I looked at your code, Gerard, it was so tangled I thought I was trying to brush out my daughter's hair."

No offence taken, Gerard smiled back. "But now we take it up a level."

Tim's eyes didn't leave the whiteboard. He scanned it twice, thrice.

"I can't make sense of this. Is this something you are planning on doing? For real? Here? With our code?"

Leo shrugged.

"For the metrics," Anna said. "It's what they want. We want to deliver."

"You said we!" Hugo's voice pulled down his face mask and grinned. "So, you are in on it!"

"Tim. We can't be dead last. If they want this, let's give them what they want."

"But what about crash rate? Incidents?"

"Leo calculated the payoff. Incidents won't go up as much as the scores we gain. It's a worthy tradeoff." Gerard pointed at a corner where Leo had presented the calculation. She had estimated that the incidents wouldn't float to the surface until at least a month later, while the score would immediately go up. They could fix the problems at a later point but still get a better placement among the teams for at least two or three weeks. At that point, maybe the incidents wouldn't even be easily traceable to them, not if they made the code complex enough, and they integrated the other APIs. That would give them another month.

"This," Tim circled the list on the whiteboard, "is everything we shouldn't be doing."

Gerard, Hugo, Anna, and Leo nodded.

"But it is what we are going to do," Leo said.

"And it would make us place better?"

"Yes."

"I'm going to regret this, aren't I?"

They looked at each other. Nobody had the heart to be honest.

"Of course not."

Tim nodded.

"I never saw this, okay?"

He left the room.

"Let's fucking do this!" Gerard clapped.

"But we start tomorrow, no?" Hugo looked at his phone. "Wife, kids, you know."

"No, we start today. We don't have a lot of time. And Hugo, my rebase master, I want you to rebase the last commits since Friday and split them up. We got to rewrite our past to write our future."

"Okay, boss. I'll call my wife first." Hugo left the room. Leo glumly glanced at her phone, seeing the many missed calls from Jack. She could see his worry and concern radiating through the device and almost wanted to laugh at how he seemed to almost hope she had an affair as it would be preferable to her burning out again. He was probably picturing her working herself into exhaustion and becoming a mere shadow of her former self - distant, tired, and overwhelmed. Leo tried to push away the thoughts and instead refocus on the great plan to survive the great merge. Jack was wrong. She'd never felt more alive. Pulse facing, ideas flowing. Just one more hour.

18

Out of breath and out of energy, Leo fell through the door and into the waiting area at the clinic. Marie stood by the coffee machine, the hum of the machine filling the otherwise silent room. She watched Leo regain composure but offered no sympathy or help.

"I'm so sorry I'm late," Leo finally said.

"You didn't get the messages?"

Leo had gotten them. All of them. More than a dozen reminders.

"I did. A few reminders." One every ten minutes for the last few hours.

"There was a little problem with the system. Ulrik, the old man, decided to do it himself. I offered to help, but he wouldn't have it." She walked to her desk, sat down, crossed her legs, and slowly stirred the black coffee with one of those useless wooden sticks.

"Modernizing, that's good!"

Marie shrugged.

"Ulrik should be out in a minute."

"Is he seeing someone?" Leo cringed at the thought of sounding like a jealous teenager. But why would he see somebody else during her time slot?

"IPS. He's at the gents."

"IBS?"

"No. IPS. Irritable Person Syndrome. He goes to the gents to vent, so I won't hear him talking to himself. The isolation is better there."

Ulrik came in, his eyebrows creased and his mouth turned downwards. He stopped when he saw Leo, his face immediately brightening up like a toddler recognizing the bag of candy behind the vegetables in the shopping bag.

"Ah, at last! You have arrived. Much-anticipated, much-awaited!"

"Sorry about that. And unfortunately, I don't have a lot of time to spare. Work is crazy right now. I just wanted to come by and say thank you."

Ulrik continued his slow walk to the office and, with a circular gesture, indicated Leo should accompany him.

"I'll have to leave in a few minutes," she reminded him.

He stopped by the window, peering out.

"It's been several days since I last heard from the pair. It prompts one to ponder - has he departed, or perhaps, has she taken leave of him?"

Leo shrugged mentally, silent as a nun.

"Esther says some people are easy to like, hard to love."

"Sounds like a bright woman."

Ulrik smiled widely, his gaze focused on the pond.

"Always has been."

They stood in silence, the sun cutting through the dim air.

"Congratulations on the scheduling system," Leo said, breaking the silence.

"You noticed! Fantastic, isn't it?"

Leo looked at the clock.

"I have to leave in five." She bit the inside of her dry, cracked lips. She had slept with her mouth open, dehydrated, and with a headache from hell. When she woke up, she felt trapped in a room with ten toddlers whose toys had no volume control. Her head was buzzing. They had stayed until late, fed only by Anna's cookies and Hugo's infallible spirit.

"Given our limited time, we better dive straight into our endeavor." Ulrik looked out the window one last time, disappointment in his eyes. He sat down with a loud, complaining squeak from the chair.

Leo had just assumed that he would want to reschedule the appointment and had only shown up to be polite. Under most circumstances, which didn't involve work, Leo was a polite person. She sat down, looked at the clock in an exaggerated manner so Ulrik would know she'd have very little time.

"I'm not sure what to say."

"You could start off by telling me how things are at work."

"Speaking of, I wanted to come here to say thank you. You said something last time when I dropped in, literally by accident, that helped me find a solution to my problem at work. Thank you for that."

"I must say, I'm not sure it's the right solution if it means you have to work even harder." He leaned forward and rubbed her knee. She shifted in her seat, but his hand remained on her knee. She observed him silently until the rubbing ceased. He withdrew his hand.

"And how is your patella?"

Leo stared at his wrinkly hand on her knee. Did he just ask her about Nutella?

"Your knee." He tapped her knee with a finger. "This is the patella."

"My knee is better, but my hearing is not very good. Head is still buzzing from a busy week."

Nutella was Jack's favorite treat. He'd buy a big tub, bury it in the corner closet in the kitchen, and take a spoon with his morning coffee and leave the spoon in the tub.

The high sugar content wouldn't allow for bacterial growth, he had explained. Leo was unconvinced.

"And how are you?" Ulrik emphasized 'you' with a thick whisper conveying concern and a reminder of the conversations they had had where the burnout had never been directly discussed, yet always present. Like a nagging reminder to take out the trash. The pile of trash had grown, and Leo was barely able to balance a banana peel on top, yet she wasn't ready to take it out. Just one more item. She was biting around the edges of her index finger. A nibble too deep, and a red dot started bleeding. She grabbed a tissue and wrapped her finger.

"A bit stressed. But not more than I can handle. It's just temporary. A little extra work. And to be fair, I've been slacking off for so long that a little bit of extra work seems only fair." Leo smiled. That was true. She had indeed been slacking off. Together with the rest of the world's software developers. With so many large enterprise companies letting engineers go, it was no wonder that Leo and everybody except Gerard was worried about their employment. Despite the impossibility of terminating someone in Sweden, a closing office was fair game in terms of letting people go. Leo hated that expression. Letting them go. As if they had been forced to stay and were finally free to leave. That it somehow would be a nice gesture.

"My last contribution was making the spinner go faster, so the clients would think the software was thinking faster."

"Still, it proved effective?"

"There were talks about a promotion," Leo deadpanned.

He raised his eyebrows, watched the crinkles in the corner of her mouth, and laughed.

"To be fair, I feel like some decisions are made by throwing darts at an idea board."

"In essence, not vastly different from my own methodologies." Ulrik offered with a wink.

Leo leaned back, let her shoulders drop, and smiled. "Maybe so."

"However, I must admit, my profession seldom demands from me an extension of the conventional working hours."

"Software developers like to compete in the Misery Olympics."

He ignored her invitation to continue the banter.

"If you persist in neglecting your well-being, refusing the necessary pauses, you're courting the risk of a recurring breakdown."

"I suppose—"

"And what might be Jack's perspective on this situation?" He caught her looking at the clock. In theory, they only had a couple of minutes left of the session, but they both knew there were no other clients booked. Leo got up, ready to leave. Although she could have stayed for a few more minutes, she wanted to get back to work.

"Jack is not thrilled about it. He says he's concerned about my mental health and that I'll work myself into a new meltdown. But I'll be fine. We'll be fine." There was little conviction in Leo's voice. Upholding her job, and consequently her pledge to Jack, held greater importance than a few dates.

Ulrik nodded sympathetically, his eyes tired.

"Consider Jack's feelings in this, Leo. Maintaining a balanced relationship is essential, especially when you're navigating such demanding work commitments. His concerns for your well-being shouldn't be dismissed lightly. Remember, we operate best not when we're merely 'fine', but when we're thriving. You've got to care for yourself in order to care for others." Ulrik looked at his desk, the yellow Post-It note with Esther on it still attached to the monitor. Esther had always been frustrated with his work ethic. He either worked too much or too little. He wondered what Esther would have said to Leo. He missed the times when they used to discuss patients. Privacy laws put a stop to that. It was very unfortunate.

"I don't think he'd leave me over it." Leo didn't mean to sound annoyed, yet the scratchy undertone of annoyance surfaced through her words. "I've got to go."

He followed her to the door.

"But you will return?"

Leo tried to open the door; however, it seemed to be locked.

"I'm not even able to leave."

"I'm sorry about that. We got these new fancy doors, and I haven't fully figured out how to operate them. When the handle is red, the door is locked." Ulrik tried pushing down the handle. It remained red, and it remained locked.

"Don't you have to unlock the door?"

"Are you suggesting that I still have to engage in the archaic practice of manually unlocking the door?"

Leo nodded.

"That certainly undermines the 'smart' in 'smart door', wouldn't you agree?" He fiddled with his phone, and a minute later, they both heard a click and the handle turned green.

"The handle is quite nice, though," Leo said, grinning before disappearing out the door.

19

Leo had been tasked with planning their date night, but deep down, she wished it wasn't her turn. It was Thursday night, and the next day the team would be reevaluated for the new metrics. There was no time for this. However, it would take longer to argue with Jack than to go through with the date night. She weighed her options and decided that fulfilling Jack's request would be the most productive use of her time. And she had a plan for getting what she wanted.

Jack was dressed up and waiting for her at home, wearing two layers of perfume and a ridiculously large smile on his face.

She had not dressed up. As a matter of fact, she had hoped she could dress down when she got home. Even though she was sporting plain jeans and a hoodie, there was room for dressing down even further. Slacks, for example, would be more comfortable than jeans.

"Well, I'm glad that you're finally spending some time at home with me. What have you planned for tonight? Is it a surprise? I love surprises!"

Leo removed her jeans, watched Jack's hopeful expression, and watched it fade as she put on the gray slacks that should have been washed two weeks ago.

"I was thinking that we could spend some time getting to know each other's hobbies."

Jack's face dimmed into a look of confusion. He wasn't sure if they had any hobbies. He had always spent all his time on his startup, so unless that would qualify as a hobby, then he didn't really have any. Playing PlayStation was something he did to kill time, but he wouldn't call it a hobby. Leo, on the other hand, liked to sleep, so in theory that could be a hobby, but it make for an immensely boring date.

"Are we staying in, or are we going out?"

Leo looked down at her slacks. They were staying in. She went through her backpack and pulled out her laptop.

"Let's start with my hobby!"

"And that would be?"

"Coding, of course!"

Jack's face dropped.

"I thought we could code together. It might be good for you to refresh your skills if you're going to act on any of your crazy app ideas," Leo replied with a cheeky smile. Jack moved away from her, leaving a gap of two people between them on the couch. Sitting at the very far end of the couch, he stared at her as if she had mewed instead of talked. Lion watched them from the corner, his tail impatiently whipping side to side.

"Are you seriously trying to get me to work on your stuff? Wait, not even *your* stuff, your work stuff. The thing I've been complaining about all week."

Leo closed the lids on the laptop. Her mission had failed. At least Jack turned out to be smarter than she thought he'd be.

"We don't have to do this. We can do something else." She dragged her words.

"No. You go ahead. Work. We'll meet up another time."

"Are you sure?"

"I'm not going to force you to do a date. It's fine. You choose, what do you want to do?"

Leo wanted to finish splitting the commits. Hugo had done his best, but with his family still being out with the flu, he hadn't been able to wrap up that part of the plan.

"I would…kind of…like to finish something…"

"Then you do that," he replied with bitterness in his voice. He got up, put on his jacket, and left.

Great! Just a couple of things left. She'd make it up to him later. And book a new appointment with Ulrik.

20

A crowd had gathered outside the building like ants in an ant stack. The dark shadows stood huddled together, shielding themselves from the harsh wind. Leo slowed down her pace as she approached them.

"What's happening?"

Hugo stepped out of the crowd. His hands in his jacket pockets, body shivering like a leaf in the wind. He explained through clattering teeth that they couldn't get in; nobody knew their key tag pin. At 7:30 in the morning, the ungodly hour they had been mandated to show up at work required a pin in addition to the key tag. Unsurprisingly, nobody had ever been in that early, not even sales. Who would they call at 7:30 in the morning?

"We're going to be late for the interrogation," Leo said through the white cloud that formed as she breathed. With arms tightly folded across her chest, she joined the huddle.

Hugo huddled closer.

"There's nothing we can do about it. Nobody from upper management is in either. They'll have to wait with the monthly until we get in. Excited about the presentation?"

She laughed without humor. Yes, the performance numbers had improved, but they were far behind the other teams. Even the Belgian team, the headless service with their mangled unfunctional functional code in obscure languages, had better metrics based on their builds.

"Promise me you won't let Jack pitch funeral apps at my funeral," she replied with a grim face. She could get lucky. Get stuck out here for the entirety of the meeting. Gregory would reschedule for next week, and she'd have more time to figure out why some tests failed intermittently. On the other side, she had spent the evening prior preparing like a cheerleader ready for her big day. Jack had said she had been practicing in her sleep, reciting building times, lines of code, and lead times. In theory, she couldn't fail with the presentation as long as she stuck to the script. In theory.

Not even five minutes later, a man of substantial size with a torso that could outshine an Olympic swimmer approached them, keys and tools rattling from a tool belt that was holding on to that last hole for dear life. One poorly planned squat and it would rip its metal organs pouring out from their practical loops and pockets. Leo deduced from his dark brown uniform, which consisted of cargo pants and a shirt with even more pockets filled to the brim, that he was a service technician. Without a word, he plowed through the crowd like Moses dividing the sea, let out a deep sigh and fell to his knees, and folded out a bag with key locks. Wasting no time, he began disassembling the lock. Unbothered by the high-pitched alarm, he replaced the lock, put a key in Leo's hand, and gestured for them to go in.

"What about the alarm?" Somebody asked.

He made a dismissive gesture with his hand and walked away, his large wingspan making him look like a bat in the night. The alarm stopped, and nobody knew why. Leo unlocked the door, and the crowd burst in, desperate to thaw. With hurried steps, they dispersed to their cells, laptops flying out of their backpacks, docking stations buzzing as they plugged in. Just before eight, the virtual room filled, awaiting Gregory's reprimand. He wasted no time. A few minutes into the lecturing, he unmuted himself and continued,

"Well, that was a disappointment. A simple request from your employer. Yet all of you managed to be late. And don't give me any of that pin nonsense. If I hadn't been working from home to avoid infecting you with this dreadful virus," he coughed into his fist like a teenager faking a sickie, "I would have held the doors open for you." He grabbed his tri-colored umbrella drink, took two small sips, and dabbed his lips with a golden-rimmed napkin.

"That's one hell of a fancy cough drink he's got there," Gerard wrote to Leo.

Judging by the color gradient and limited nightlife experience, Leo deduced that it was a Tequila Sunrise. Gregory took another sip, looked at the glass with a look of realization on his face, and moved the glass outside the frame. He had chosen a static background with a mock office matching his crisp white shirt and neatly combed hair. He looked like a realtor from one of those reality shows where they sell billion-dollar homes.

"Let's not waste more time." Gregory paused to roll his eyes. "The Björking Dogs, you are first."

The Icelandic team, which consisted of a sole developer, probably the only one on the island, a database administrator, and five designers delivered a flatlined presentation with metrics typed in Notepad.

"Thank you, metrics are looking better. Well done!"

Jón's face showed no emotion. He blinked twice, stopped screen-sharing, and turned his camera off. His profile picture looked identical and just as lively as the real-life version of him. In quick succession, the teams delivered their results with shaky voices, over-engineered PowerPoint outsourced to unemployment project leaders, and one by one, the cameras were turned off.

Gregory brought back his drink, and the background glitched as he took a long sip. "Next time, let's do this in person. Iceland is close to Sweden, isn't it? It's all Scandinavia, right?"

"What does that even mean?" Gerard wrote to Leo.

"That the optional in-person is not optional."

"What the hell? Is he growing horns?"

Leo laughed. Gerard could be ruder than an annoyed teenager, but he was entertaining. Gregory reached for the glass again, and that's when Leo saw it. The background glitched again. Behind Gregory was a tropical beach—the expensive type. Maldives, Bahamas. Not the depressive beaches Leo had visited in the UK or the seagull-shit-covered rocks in Sweden. This was at least two layovers away. Mandated to go in on a Monday, at 7:30 AM, during a baby snowstorm, to remote into a moody CEO drinking fancy drinks in the Bahamas. Leo's blood boiled. She grabbed a screenshot of the meeting. Gregory's face froze as he took another sip, his lips stuck to the glass like a tongue stuck to a lamppost. She drew red horns on him and sent the screenshot to Gerard.

"You're up," Gerard wrote in the chat.

"You can do it, Leo!" Hugo wrote.

"Hi. Right. Right." Leo's anxiety ran her over like a freight train. She adopted the posture of a forgotten tomato plant and the vocabulary of a three-year-old toddler.

"So. Yes. We are the Cock— Sorry. Cogwheels." She shared the first slide with the glowing balls. "Sorry. Wrong logo. I couldn't find the cogwheels."

"I can tell." Gregory fake-laughed. "Something is not quite right up there."

"Here are the team results," Leo continued, unfazed. What's the worst that can happen? She straightened up and cleared her throat. A lot could go wrong, but as Ulrik said, we are all born with the capacity to make mistakes, but at least we made something.

121

She shared a colorful slide and delivered her triumphant speech.

"…and our best metric, Lines of Code, has improved by 20%. The wheels are turning, and we are churning out code like there's no tomorrow." One slide to go. Leo exhaled, and the corners of her mouth pulled up and out. Nearly a smile.

"Unfortunately, Leo, you seem to have missed the meeting last night. And you've also missed that no other team reported lines of code. I'm feeling particularly generous today, so I'll give us a little refresher. I took a look at the code in all three products, and there's a lot of it. We are at almost 300,000 lines of code for something that should at most take 20,000 lines. It's too complex. Hardly makes any sense. Anybody should be able to open any file and understand what the code does. It makes no sense. Does it have to be so complicated? No. We are just comparing prices. It's simple math. We are going to have to rewrite. Rewrite everything."

"Parts of it? The infrastructure? Or do you mean sit down and start from scratch?" Hugo asked in the chat.

"A rewrite. It's too complex!" Gregory responded.

"Hi. I'm sorry. I… I don't understand what's too complex. Can you explain? Maybe I'm just…" Hugo's voice cracked as his confidence faltered.

"All of it. Just look at it."

Gregory drained the glass and waved to somebody offscreen. "Look." He took over the screen sharing. "It's too much stuff." He scrolled through a deployment script. "There's no price comparison here, is there?" A new drink appeared in a corner. "And I bet you I could go to our server hall and unplug a server, and nothing would happen. Because we have hundreds of servers, and I bet only a third of them are actually doing anything. You know what that is called?"

Silence.

"Server hoarding. That's what it's called. You know the show, Hoarders? Filthy people, with no better life ambitions than to renovate homes into junkyards—"

"It's a show about mental prob—"

Whoever said that was quickly disposed of.

"Should I say something about the fail-over cluster?" Leo typed to Gerard but maintained eye contact with the camera. She waited for the ping and looked down.

"Are you on drugs? For God's sake, no!"

"Leo? Leo! The stage is yours unless you were done?" Gregory said.

Leo hit the screen-sharing button again and selected her monitor.

"And to summarize if we ignore the—"

"Is that me?" Gregory hissed.

Leo looked at the screen. No. It was a slide. The summary slide. And the other screen, framed by a lime green box that indicated screen sharing was the screenshot of the meeting, with a horn-decorated Gregory.

"And are those horns?"

She had shared the wrong screen.

"NO!" Leo shouted. "It's…it's cat ears. I wanted to share a fun picture from this meeting with all of us, like cats. Like the musical, Cats."

"And why would you do that?" Gregory growled the words.

"I'm, I'm a crazy cat lady. I like cats. *A lot.*"

"And you have how many cats, exactly?"

"One."

"Not many for a crazy cat lady."

"They wouldn't let me have more than one. I'm on a special list."

"You are special all right." Gregory looked at his Cartier watch. "Saved by the bell. 9:30. I believe we have our Scrum of Scrums of Scrums. Leo, I'll call you after SSS."

21

Leo decided to go to her safe place. Not the bathroom, but the other place. The cat café.

She recounted her options as she waded through the wet, brown snow on the side street, her jeans soaking up the dirty water like tea bags in old tea.

Option one: go home and listen to Jack's app ideas. Possible secondary outcome: Jack would tell her he was right, and she had been wrong.

Option two: move abroad, maybe Thailand.

Option three: cat café.

"Hello, Sash?"

Through the thick air of feline wonder Sasha appeared, like a cat goddess with her servants circling her feet with soft tails and pointy whiskers.

"Hey, Sash. I need Marshmallow. Is Marshmallow in?"

"I'm sorry, Leo, but Marshmallow is not available right now. Can I offer you a different cat? Maybe two cats?"

It felt wrong to be there. Leo could have been at home with Lion instead, but Lion wouldn't understand. He wasn't that type of cat, and he couldn't give her what she needed. She needed affection, cuddles. All of it. And she needed it now. Before her life would come to a close. At least her life in Sweden.

"I'm having a really bad day, so I'll take anything that you got, as long as it's a cuddly one."

Sasha smiled wide and waved her in and whispered, "I've got everything that you need, trust me. There is something for everybody here." She winked. Leo's morals were up for sale. At least according to Lion.

Leo followed her into the innermost corner, where her usual spot was waiting for her.

It felt like it was only a day ago that she had been there with Gerard. She sat down, slumped over in defeat. The Marshmallow substitute was a ragdoll with gray fur and blue eyes and an orange cat of unknown origin and race. Sasha made good on her promise. Both cats were more than happy to sit on Leo's lap, purring happily as she stroked their shiny fur. She would have to remember to wash her hands and face, change her sweater, and remove her jacket before she went home. If Lion were to find out, she'd be in big trouble.

"Is there anything else you would like?" Sasha gave Leo a sympathetic smile but didn't wait for an answer before she left, her smaller servants demanding her attention. Leo leaned back and closed her eyes, petting the cats slowly. She must have fallen asleep because she woke to loud, agitated voices. She couldn't quite place the agitated voice. Male British. Youthful. Cocky. She couldn't make out the words, but the person, the man, was arguing with Sasha. Leo put down the cats gently, as to avoid offending them for interrupting the cuddling session, and went to find out what the commotion was about.

"Jack, what are you doing here?"

Jack was standing by the door gesturing wildly with his arms contrasted by an indifferent Sasha.

"Leo, tell her to let me in!" he pleaded.

"Let him in. The idiot is my boyfriend."

"Idiot-boyfriend, *welcome* in." Sasha said the word 'welcome' tasting of lime.

They waded through the cats and sat down by the table. The ragdoll eyed Jack up and down before settling in on Leo's lap again. Jack didn't like cats; cats didn't like him. It was a fair deal.

"Are you hiding?"

"Maybe. Are you stalking?"

"You won't believe this, but there's this new app I've been working on. With the help of AI, it helps you figure out where people in your life are."

"Not even I know where I'm in life."

"Not metaphorically, but where they are physically. On a map."

"A tracking app."

"It's not really tracking. It's a calculation. You know, AI."

"I don't know AI, but you do seem to be very fond of him."

"Or her." Jack winked. Leo groaned.

Out of all the ridiculous ideas Jack had had, this would absolutely be in the top ten. Placing among ten might seem like a low number, but with Jack's many ideas, it would be a high rating in stupidity. If it had been any other day, Leo would have roasted Jack over the idea, but she had no energy.

"Is everything okay at work?"

"No…"

Leo told Jack about Gregory and work, and his reaction was exactly what she had expected.

"I told you, as long as they have investors, they have to prove what they are doing. You can't just trick them into keeping the office if there's no reason for the office to exist. I don't want to be rude, but if somebody else can do what your team is doing, and they can do it better, is it really that crazy that they would want to replace the team?"

127

"Whose side are you on?"

"You have to do better or do differently." Jack tried to pick up a black cat, but it hissed back.

"That cat is not on the menu." Leo nodded at the brochure on the table. It listed the cats, a short presentation, and ratings for petting, purring, and heat generation. Similar to the way wines are rated, but instead scoring sweetness, bitterness, and other characteristics. The black cat was labeled as off-limits. It was the head cat.

"Aren't you worried about how Lion is going to react? You going to other cats?" Jack commented after a while.

"Nah. What would he do about it?"

22

Leo checked their message channel first thing in the morning. First thing in the morning meant 10AM. She expected the team to lament about their score, but they were more concerned about the team logo and how it rendered on a light background. Since they weren't serial killers, and therefore used a dark background for everything, none of them had tried the logo on a white background. The cogwheels, or balls, were barely visible, and the glow was nonexistent.

Leo: Any thoughts on the performance score.

Gerard: I'd say we fucking aced it.

Gerard: But the wrong side of the scale.

Leo: We'd place better if it wasn't for Gregory changing the metrics.

Hugo: We know we are good, boss. We don't need numbers to prove that.

Leo: It's sort of the whole point of the performance metrics.

Gerard: Which is bullshit.

Anna: I agree with Hugo.

Leo: Aren't you guys upset?

Anna: It's just numbers. Like Hugo says, we are good at what we do.

Gerard: And it can't be measured with fucking random metrics.

Hugo: The metrics aren't random. *True randomness is the concept of generating numbers, data, or events that are truly unpredictable and lack any discernible pattern.*

Gerard: Fucking Christ, you are obstinate. Did you copy-paste that from somewhere on the internet?

Hugo: No.

Gerard: You left the formatting.

Hugo: My point stands. The metrics aren't random. You are such a Sangrón.

Gerard: Is the Mexican saying Mexican things again?

Anna: He is saying you are annoying.

Leo: None of you care at all about being dead last?

Gerard: Now *you* are being annoying.

Like a child that had been told off, Leo left the channel. It would say *Leo left the channel.* And they'd be worried and ask if she was okay. And she'd say, *No, I'm not okay. And you shouldn't be okay!*

She waited. Watched the screen intently. And waited again. Nothing. She closed the laptop hard, as if slamming a door but without the intended dramatic effect. Her blood was seething like a volcano, threatening to erupt. It was unfathomable that they didn't care about the result of their efforts - weren't they the least bit proud? Or did someone rip their pride out and throw it into a trash can? *Okay. Calm down.* She looked at herself in the mirror. *Maybe*

I can still save this. A foul smell tickled her nose. The odor came from the hallway. A place that usually had no odor. She sniffed her way along the walls. In the jackets. The odor lingered in the air but did not give any hints about its whereabouts. A ghostly smell. The shoes. Maybe she had stepped in shit. To be fair. It was hard to tell the difference between the snow and dog shit. The color was the same.

And there it was.

Inside her white sneaker.

A turd. A Lion turd.

Lion had taken a dump in her shoes.

There were two questions. How had he been able to aim so well, and why would he do such a thing. Lion was watching her. A smirk beaded with his whiskers. He knew about the other cats.

She cleaned out the turd and chucked her shoe in the washing machine. Watching the shoe toss around, banging against the metallic walls, soothed her boiling blood. She'd have to go to work in an hour for their morning meeting. She let the shoe continue spinning with five hours left of the eco-friendly cycle. At least it would use less water. But more electricity.

23

The blaring sound and intense red light that flooded the room violated Leo's senses. Covering her ears, she watched the confusion as the team demonstrated how utterly useless they'd be if there was a fire. For example, that one time they decided the lamp in the corner, the only halogen lamp, was too bright and therefore covered it with a beanie, which later smoked into a cozy fire. They had to endure sub-zero temperatures for a week while the smell found its way out the windows and the roasted polyester aroma dissolved. Leo had been quite fond of the smell. It reminded her of fresh keyboards.

The yearly fire drill was ignored by the software teams, but this was the second drill in less than two months, which meant it could be a real fire. Gerard shrugged, put on his headphones, and sat back down. He was going down with the ship, Titanic style, but he'd have his favorite tune playing while being engulfed. Spice Girls. He would never admit to it, but they all knew it.

With a triumphant grin, Hugo beckoned them over.

"It's not a fire drill! It's our new Daily Standup light! Look!" He pointed to the large rotating light that spun around a strobe of red light that matched the pulsating blare.

"Can you turn that fucking thing off?" Gerard's voice could barely be heard.

Hugo had programmed the light to run for the duration of the meeting. Twenty minutes. He couldn't unplug it as it was connected directly to a power outlet that also powered their build server, and the current build had at least four hours left.

"TIME FOR DAILY STANDUP!" Like a stealthy ninja, Tim had snuck in.

"SORRY I'M LATE. CAN WE START? HUGO TURN IT OFF!"

Anna, Leo, and Gerard joined Tim by the whiteboard. They had run out of sanitizer when they had attempted to remove the master plan, and the drawing of Gregory was still there. Anna had tried to cover it up by adding to it, and Gregory was, according to the new drawing, standing in a music store. With a CD in his hand. Hugo had, of course, drawn a shark at the bottom, which Gerard had violently crossed out.

"I'll use the app to turn it off." Hugo looked at his phone. The app was grayed out. He'd had to download it again.

"TURN OFF!" Hugo yelled at his phone. "SIRI, TURN OFF!"

"Turning on *Get off lights*."

"Get off?"

The phone assistant returned. "Could not *Get off. Sexy time* failed to launch."

"It's the smart lights at home. Night light for the twins." Hugo explained, red-faced.

"*Get off?*"

"We repurposed our bedroom lights."

"I don't even want to know." Gerard chuckled.

"Voice commands seem to turn off a siren seems like a bad match," Anna shouted.

The sound stopped. The room regained its gray color.

"I can't believe you were able to turn it off with voice commands!" Anna beamed with enthusiasm.

"Oh. It stopped because it's twenty past. I wasn't able to make it stop. But I will tomorrow. *Yo prometon.*"

"Please don't tell me you spent a lot of time on this…" Leo moaned. It would explain why he hadn't created as many commits as she had instructed him to, but she knew better than to bring it up now.

Hugo had spent half a day. But it had been worth it. It was a beautiful light. The best light. And fun side projects were known to boost morale. At least according to a TEDX talk he had watched during a bathroom break.

"Hugo? Are you with us?" Leo was drawing an aubergine on the whiteboard. The Belgian team had chosen the vegan favorite as their logo and used it unironically, albeit its euphemistic appearance. It was a problematic team. The Aubergine team belonged to a former competitor, but Leo's team was expected to become close-knit overnight similar to a sibling being forced to accept and love a sweaty potato newly brought home from the hospital.

"I don't get it. Why an eggplant?" Anna blushed.

"It's an aubergine," Gerard insisted.

"No, eggplant."

"It's called an *aubergine*," Gerard enunciated each word slowly and with an exaggerated French accent that he had saved for occasions like this.

"Is it like squash versus zucchini?"

"*Courgette*," Gerard retorted.

"I just don't understand why they'd use a phallic vegetable as their logo."

"Aren't all vegetables phallic?"

"Not onions."

Nobody would use an onion as a team logo.

"Speaking of, we should use the onion pattern for our next service," Anna added. She had been to another conference and returned with another idea.

"Is it called onion pattern because the more you peel back the layers, the more you cry?"

"Look, guys." Leo removed the 'aubergine or zucchini' note on the whiteboard. "We are supposed to use some of their stuff for our calculations."

"Did we get any more information, boss? How are we reusing?"

"No more than that. There's no API, no separate library. It's a spaghetti bowl, and Gregory is under the impression that we can just shove our hands into the bowl and grab a meatball for our plate although the code is more tightly coupled than Siamese twins."

The Belgian team owned the former competitor's algorithm for price comparison, and somehow the two services had to be magically unified. Same for the Icelandic team, but they seemed to focus solely on the design aspect of the web application.

Tim put on his best cheerleader face. "Look at it from this perspective. With more people on the team, we'll get more done! Faster!"

"You sound like a project manager." Gerard chuckled and ignored the subsequent death stare. "I'm sure you know, Tim, that nine women can't give birth in a month."

"Ten months. It's ten months for a baby," Anna said quietly from her corner.

Hugo nodded in agreement. "If you ask my wife, it feels like twenty months."

Anna rearranged the cookies. She had placed the variety of cookies on a three-tier cake stand. The bottom was filled with colorful macarons, Leo's favorite. The top tier, with only four strange-looking cookies, was the gluten-free-vegan-no-sugar-organic-fair-trade-cocoa cookies. They'd been there for a week; nobody had wanted them.

Tim threw a glance at the cookies. They were calling his name.

Hugo shrugged and pulled out a dusty, dark gray laptop covered in miniature fingerprints. Ten hobbits had fought and lost the battle of the laptop. Hugo sighed, "It's old, I know. But it's up to date and spins."

"I'm not judging." Leo pointed out the twin laptop on the desk. "I'm just happy I'm not the only one with museum equipment. Although I was hoping it would increase in value as a retro artifact. You just lowered its value if yours starts."

"Don't worry. My kids have a personal vendetta against anything I claim as mine. It's only a matter of time before they find a way to fit it in the toilet or their breakfast bowl." Hugo pointed out the incriminating evidence, the prints.

"The link for the repository is in the channel. Luc finally sent us the link."

Hugo clicked the link, grabbed the URL, and cloned the repository locally. They waited.

"It's… a bit slow?"

"Took me ten minutes. It's a monorepo." Leo shrugged. She had downloaded the code while she waited for them to finish playing.

Tim raised an eyebrow. Leo explained, "Monorepos are the equivalent of keeping all your candy in one giant bowl - it's delicious to have instant, widespread access to anything you could want, but eventually things get muddled together, and you can't tell what's what."

"No fancy microservices then?" Tim asked.

"Depends on who you ask. But mono just refers to them having everything in one place." Leo leaned forward and pointed at Hugo's screen. He was clicking through the folders, and there were a lot of them.

"I'm not sure where to go. The screaming is very distracting." The folders were in all caps, COMPARE-THE-P-.

"Compare the pee?"

"Compare the price. I'm guessing the paths got too long, and they had to shorten the prefix. But what do I know? It's better than our name, P and P. It sounds like pee-pee. There's the solution file. Run it."

The Visual Studio logo appeared on the screen, but that was it. Hugo clicked once, twice, thrice, a hundred times. Nothing.

"Rage clicking?" Gerard circled the table again. "Doesn't have the same effect on a laptop keyboard. You got to use a mechanical keyboard if you really want to rage. Or proper mouse. Not that nipple square."

"Nipple square?"

"You rub it like a nipple." Gerard demonstrated in the palm of his hand.

Anna sighed. "I don't even want to know how you came up with that, Gerard, but never rub a nipple like that. Not even your own."

Leo gasped at Anna's uncharacteristic comment.

"Want to grab a coffee while we wait?" Hugo nodded toward the laptop. The program was grayed out. "*Not responding*, boss."

"I guess some things never change." Anna sighed and continued in a squeaky voice, "*Would you like to wait for the program to respond?*"

"No!" Leo laughed. "It's a trick question I've been told. Leave it."

They waited. The waiting consisted of getting two cups of coffee, a Snickers bar from the snack drawer, making awkward small talk, and going for a 20-minute walk around the building to absorb some sunrays.

They returned to a fuming laptop and an angry, red error window, yelling at them about everything that was wrong. Everything was wrong. The editor had turned into a teenager.

Hugo squinted. "There are 2390 errors. Is this our new normal? I thought Luc's stuff was made out of glitter and unicorns."

Leo peered over his shoulder. "Shouldn't be that many. I only have about 50."

"Why do I have so many, then?"

"Did you filter to ignore editor errors? I just ignored them." Leo shrugged. Hugo filtered, and 50 errors remained.

"Intelligent code completion errors aren't genuine errors. It's like a drunk friend giving advice. Sometimes they might have a point, but usually, it's just gibberish."

"Can we sober up our drunken friend?"

"Sure, just delete the solution file." Gerard reached out for the trackpad, but Hugo slapped his hand away.

"Lay off my nipple, creep. I'll just ignore them for now. What about the other 50 errors?"

Leo grinned. "Just ignore those as well."

"It won't build if I do. They are *real* errors."

"Exclude the Engine project from the solution. We don't need that project anyway," Leo replied with a shrug.

"Why is it there, then?"

"I don't know. But it won't build with it," Leo added, "obviously."

"So, this," Hugo stared at the nipple square, "is our normal?"

"Yes." Leo gave a thumbs-up and a big grin. "We have become one with the Belgian team. *Mi case, su casa.*"

"Gracias," Hugo whispered, defeated.

Leo continued, "And like the song goes, I've got 99 errors but the build ain't one."

"If you are having build problems, I feel bad for you, son. I got 99 problems but the build ain't one. Hit me!" The lyrics had been on repeat during Hugo's youthful years, when he had worked as a bartender at a tropical bar in San Diego. He'd give anything, except maybe his kids and wife, to be there now soaking up the sun like an oil-covered former Baywatch star.

Leo brought him back to reality with a fist firmly punching his left shoulder.

"¡Basta!"

Leo had no idea why he would yell '*saunaing*' in Swedish but attributed his outburst to culture differences and a sudden urge to return to tropical temperatures. It would be several months and even more sauna outbursts before Leo, with a smidge of embarrassment, realized that it meant *enough* in Spanish.

24

The biohazardous experiment confined in a robust IKEA lunchbox made of glass reminded Leo why she shouldn't bring her own lunch. Without failure, she'd forget the lunch box in her backpack or the fridge. Subsequently, a righteous individual would publicly shame her for the self-sustained ecosystem, but only when they were certain it wasn't kimchee, kombucha, or douche. A green mushroom cloud, spongy and dotted with black, was unmistakably not a cultural delicacy.

By the coffee machine, four colleagues stood cackling like hens, discussing where they would get lunch. Leo avoided eye contact as she poured her cup and tuned in to their recommendations, which sounded akin to organizing a trip.

"Indian!" one cackled.

"No, Chinese!" the other one insisted.

"Vietnamese! Mexican!"

As two people didn't want Asian food, they circled back to the idea of Indian cuisine. Should she tell? They either simply didn't know or had perfectly good reasons to ignore India's location on the world map. Nothing good would come out of a remark, so Leo said she'd join them and made sure to stay two steps behind the flock as they bobbed down the stairs, their heads eerily steady as the body moved. She had seen this on video, how a hen could be moved but its head remain fixed. Vestibulo-ocular reflex, a reflex particularly important for animals that rely on vision for survival. Much like software developers waiting for a build to succeed. Everybody knew that averting your gaze would make the build fail.

They fell out the door and into the restaurant on the bottom floor, which they'd been able to smell for the last two hours. The ventilation guy, Rob-something, had investigated and concluded that the restaurant's ventilation system was connected with theirs, and at 10AM when they fired up the curry in the big pans, the aromatic smells got sucked in and subsequently found their way to the office. Despite their pleading emails, the landlord didn't address the problem.

Leo dodged the hens' questions about her profession. Instead, she informed them that she was a programmer. Without failure, that piece of information made her an alien, and they nodded politely and moved on with their cackling while they made their way back upstairs.

"I swear," red-haired Leanne said while they walked up the stairs, their breath left behind at the first floor, "if we move offices, I won't stick around. I live and breathe for the food variety on this street." The others nodded.

"And everybody knows the restaurants that offer foods from any corner of the world is a lie. Like, you can do sushi, meatballs, Pho, *and* curry? Nah. I don't buy it. Don't get me wrong, I like the idea. Who wouldn't? But that's just crazy." She leaned against the wall, breathing heavily, and let the tall blonde woman push open the door.

They held the door open for Leo, but she stood frozen by the stairs, glaring at the open door. They waited for an awkward minute, shrugged, and let the door close shut.

Multiple languages, Leo thought. That's it. She had to tell the team.

She tugged at the door handle, but it wouldn't budge. Great. Her tag was on her desk. She called Anna, who had just finished handing out a fresh batch of cookies in the kitchen.

"We are going to rewrite our services in several languages. Like an amazing puzzle made from micro-languages. And before you say no," Leo had noticed Gerard massaging his temples, and Hugo whispering *no*, "just imagine. Developers adding or working on our services can pick and choose their preferred language, suited for their needs and expertise, and they can also blend elements from multiple languages to come up with creative solutions. In other words, they will have an almost unlimited supply of tools at their disposal - perfect for making sure that programming projects run as smoothly as possible."

"Sounds like a bad idea, boss. Sorry. Shouldn't we just focus on merging services?" Hugo patted Leo on her shoulder. An empathetic move contrasted by Gerard's outburst.

"You are insane. Fucking insane. Have you been watching Big Data conference sessions again? Fucking insane."

"Polyamory service sounds fun though," Anna said.

"*Polyglot*. It's called polyglot. Polyamory is like a buffet but with relationships instead of food. A polyglot service is a clusterfuck of languages where the sex is bad, nobody gets off, and you can't even sell the video," Gerard said, preaching his truth.

"I didn't know you make porno, G!" Hugo's shoulders shook as he laughed, oblivious to Gerard's red face.

"Let's just do it as a fun exercise. A break from the ordinary," Leo suggested. "There's never been a successful merge, and even if there could be, it would take too long."

"Better get started, then, boss. With the merge."

"And," Leo added, "if the merge goes too well, don't you think they'd trim the teams to save money?"

"Did they say that? Does that happen?" Hugo grabbed Leo by the arm.

"No, don't worry," Leo lied. "I'm just saying, let's have some fun while we wait for Luc to look at our code and tell us more about what's wrong with it. It's going to take ages just to get the requirements from management. They don't even know what they want, besides a *merge*."

Hugo let go of her arm.

"Just for fun?" Despite Gerard's hostile stare, Anna tried to adopt a conciliatory tone.

"Just for fun," Leo said, her sweaty hands hidden in her pockets. It could be fun, of course. But fun was not what she was looking for. If the Belgian team got points for their *Look at me, I'm written in Rust and I'm all fancy*-service, then Gregory would have a mindgasm when he'd see their polyglot baby.

"Just for fun." She smiled and nodded vigorously. Gerard did not look like he was up for the fun.

"Didn't you say you wanted to try out Rust, Gerard?" Anna winked at Leo. Gerard signed deeply. He had. He wasn't sure why, or what exactly he would do with the knowledge, but Rust was oh-so-hot-right-now and nerdiest of the nerdiest language to speak. Like Japanese had been back in the days before it was surpassed by Korean and that God-awful pop music that Anna absolutely loved. He blamed it on the sushi. Sushi became mainstream, and a decade later people finally removed the spell of vinegar and seaweed and saw that they were just eating rice with tiny pieces of protein on it. They had to find something else, and Korea was something else.

"So, I get to use Rust?"

Leo nodded. "Elevator language for you!"

"Oh! Can I use Go?"

Leo nodded again.

"With TinyGo? And ItsyBitsyGo?" Hugo couldn't contain his excitement. It poured through his glazed eyes.

"If there's an AtomGo and ProtonGo, use those as well."

"And Haskell?" Anna matched Hugo's enthusiasm. The room went silent.

"Because math. That's what we do."

"Sure," Leo confirmed with another nod.

"And CoffeeScript," Gerard added.

"Dead and buried. We are not digging up that monster."

"I'm just fucking with you."

"All right. Let's do it then!"

"Now? We have to present our service to Gregory tomorrow. We won't have time to fix the issues with the API."

Their API never returned any error codes. Instead, they always returned 200, because it seemed more positive, but with an error message if there was an error. Akin to a shit sandwich, Tim had explained, "Rather than just delivering the bad news directly, you wrap it between two 'slices' of more positive information. This helps soften the blow and make the overall experience easier to swallow." Leo insisted they would still know they ate shit, but Tim wouldn't budge. The 200 wouldn't be like a pat on the back congratulating them for making an API request. But the error message would tell them that, albeit with good intention and excellent execution, the call was wrong for one of many reasons. The reasons were represented by error codes that had to be looked up, though. Leo guessed it, another API call.

"He won't mind." Leo bit her lip. Lying was not her thing.

"He seems like somebody that would mind," Gerard said slowly.

Gerard stared at Leo, sensing something wasn't right. Leo folded her hands, staring at them in her lap. A tiny lie.

A lie may take care of the present, but it has no future, Jack used to say. Meh.

"As a matter of fact, I talked to Gregory. He loved the idea."

"Really, boss?"

"Really, Hugo." Leo stood up, clapped once, and with a confident stride walked to her desk. "Are we doing this?"

Like most programmers do, Leo had underestimated work by a mile. It was more than they could chew off, but she was not going to be the one to admit it.

This could possibly be, she admitted to herself, the biggest blunder she could have ever made. It was a famous trait amongst programmers all over the world to underestimate the amount of work required for any given task. Maybe she should feel proud to follow in the footsteps of other great programmers. She looked at Gerard. His eagerness had turned into quiet drowsiness. He had skipped his afternoon nap and remained glued to his monitors where Rust documentation was neatly organized with colorful tabs. He had spent half an hour writing the script for color coding the tabs, but he insisted it was time well spent.

Anna had emptied the freezer and thawed the last batch of cookies to keep them sugared up and working. Combined with caffeine, they had managed to stay awake and productive. But the clock was ticking. Hours had flown by with no visible progress. Leo watched them one by one, increasing the swearing per minute metrics. A telltale sign of frustration. It was seven, and mentions of dinner surfaced. Dinner at home, not in the office, in front of the computer. The code wasn't even compiling, but they were so close, she could feel it. She looked over at Hugo. He had glanced at his phone every minute. The constant stream of fun photos of his kids had stopped, and the

145

messages were getting shorter until they completely stopped. He had a family waiting for him back home, yet he remained glued to his chair despite the urge to reach out for them. All he wanted was to rush back home before it got too late, but here he still was - typing away at his keyboard. Leo probed her heart, trying to find guilt. There was none. Caffeine, adrenaline, and obsession had chased it away.

This was going to be her moment, she thought as she looked at the remaining lines of code on her screen. It would be worth it.

"It's getting late, and I got to go home to my family, boss." He wanted to go home and see his children before they fell asleep, he explained.

"Do they go to bed at eight? Seems very early. They don't need that much sleep." Despite the humor in her voice, he didn't seem amused or entertained.

"I'm going home. I see you tomorrow?"

She could have nodded, said something polite. Thanked him for staying late, for pushing on. But she was too focused, and all he got in response to his polite goodbye was her head bobbing over the keyboard.

"Can you fix the calculation controller when the kids have gone to bed?" She didn't look up from her computer.

"¿Perdón?"

"Can you fix…"

"I heard. But I said I'm done for today."

"Just a little? Five more minutes?" She turned around and winked. Five more minutes for a programmer could be hours.

"No, I'm done," Hugo said in a short tone and started packing up his things.

"Two minutes?"

As he lifted his head to face her, his eyes narrowed and darkened, a visible contradiction to his usual cheerful demeanor.

146

"Leo. It's enough. Don't you have somewhere else to be? Your stay-at-home husband? No?"

Jack had called Leo several times, but she hadn't picked up. If she answered, she knew she'd get an earful; therefore, the most sensible thing to do was to not pick up. It was like Schroeder's cat. As long as she didn't acknowledge she had let Jack down, the situation existed in a state of potential. He could be upset, or not be upset. The only thing she knew was that she had to finish what she started.

She looked at Hugo. "Go home. I'll figure this out." She sighed and looked away from Hugo's accusing eyes. It was too late for apologies now, so she just nodded and said, "Go home to your family."

Anna was the next one to leave. She was quiet throughout the evening, as she often was while writing code. Nevertheless, she collected her possessions and announced her departure. She had a show she wanted to watch. A cooking show.

"Did you finish?" Leo asked, half-expecting Anna to stay and help her out.

"No," she replied without waiting for an answer. "I'm done for today." She grabbed her laptop and left.

Jack: Leo? Can you at least let me know that you are safe? Not dead in a ditch?

Even if you are dead, can you at least let me know? Just a short message, hey I'm dead. So I know?

Leo had no choice but to reply to Jack's message. Tempted to write that she was dead, she concluded that he was not up for jokes.

Leo: No, I'm safe. But it's getting late, and I still have a lot of work to do.

147

She looked up from her phone as she heard Gerard yawning loudly. The exhaustion was beginning to take its toll on him. He had finally fallen asleep at his desk, lulled by the sound of keyboards and code. Leo took a deep breath as she looked around the room: Hugo left in anger, Anna left with a quiet goodbye and Gerard slumped over in his chair - all gone, every one of them leaving her alone in the office. Abandoned. She shook her head and went back to work.

She pushed away thoughts of Jack at home, waiting for her. This was going to take all night and maybe into the morning, too. At least they had bedrooms in the office now. Surprisingly, the most affordable bed at IKEA ended up being their best-selling one.

"Fucking sharks!" Gerard shrieked and shot up, his eyes wide open.

"It's a dream, Gerard," Leo said softly.

He nodded, realizing what was happening, and looked around the room.

"Ahhh…" He muttered, still a little confused. "We're all alone."

"They left. But we are so close. I need you."

Gerard seemed unfazed by her pleading words and got up to pack his things.

"No, I'm done," he said with a grunt.

Leo stared at him, angry and disappointed, close to tears.

"Come on, Leo," Gerard said softly, realizing the situation.

"We all have our limits. Okay? This is my fucking limit. And it should be yours as well. We don't get paid for overtime; you know?"

"Money isn't everything," Leo said and immediately regretted the platitude.

"Tell my mortgage that," Gerard said sarcastically, stuffing his laptop in the bag. "Go to bed, Leo. We have all

148

done our part." He slung the bag over his back and walked out of the room, leaving her alone with her thoughts and doubts.

She looked around at the empty office - it was almost eerie now that everyone had left. She took a deep breath. Just a quick nap in the communal bedroom. Just five minutes.

25

In an office building in downtown Gothenburg, a high pitch sound easily recognized as an intruder alarm woke up the city at 7:34 AM. Paul always chose the early shift as there were rarely any calls. He'd gotten into the habit of having a dual breakfast, one at five AM and another at seven. Technically, the second breakfast didn't break fast, but he had never bothered with technicalities. Between the first and second breakfast, he'd play PlayStation, scroll on social media, making sure to remain unsocial. By 8, he could get some laundry done, and at nine plan brunch. The buzzing work phone, the size of a brick from the 80s, rang for half a minute before he realized that it was not a daydream. This was the second early call this month. He'd have to change his strategy. He looked at the phone. No shit. Same place as last time. He threw on his jacket and with a sigh left out the door. Some fucker had triggered the alarm or left a window ajar. In the same vein as the halogen lamp incident.

Leo woke with a dry mouth and dreams of a desert. She squinted at the inexplicable light pouring through the window that she had opened last night. Why so bright now at night? She pulled the covers over her head, shielding her face from the light and the cold air. And what the hell was up with the loud siren? Probably Hugo's hobby project malfunctioning.

"Turn the thing off!" She yelled, muffled by the covers. "Turn off *Get off*. TURN OFF *SEXY TIME!*"

"Mam?"

Paul stared at the covers forming an erect tent.

"Yes?" the covers replied.

"I'm from Securities. The alarm went off."

"Can you turn it off?"

"Yes. But it takes a minute." The sound disappeared mid-sentence, and the word minute came out as loud and aggressive.

"I promise I'll set the alarm before I leave tonight." Leo wasn't showing her face, but the air had gotten stale and hot under the covers.

"It's morning, mam."

"Morning?"

"I'll have to report this."

"Please don't!" Leo softened her voice and pleaded to the empty room. "Hello?"

Paul had left so he could finish his second breakfast. He had gotten used to his bi-hourly feed and hurried home, his stomach growling. Leo, looking disheveled, wiped the sleep from her eyes and prepared herself for the morning light.

What time was it?

What had happened?

She was going to sleep for five minutes. Five developer minutes, but nonetheless, it couldn't be morning. She looked out the window; the wind slapping her cheeks. People lined the sidewalks like ants, keeping a perfect social distance of a meter and a half from the next person. It was morning. Her phone was dead. She hurried to her desk. No charger. Fine. She didn't want to deal with Jack right now, anyway. She heard voices by the entrance. Sales. This meant Gregory and his crew would be next. And the first thing on the calendar was the meeting with Leo's team.

With weak legs, she half-jogged to the kitchen, hoping to find the remains of the communal breakfast. The one Gregory had canceled.

Snacks.

She could get some snacks instead. The drawers were empty. They had stopped the snacks as well.

Okay. Just water then.

She'd get water and then a coffee. She turned on the faucet. Nothing. They canceled water? She closed and opened the faucet, lifting the leveler to maximum position. The position, which someone with a creative touch had sketched on the wall, was adjacent to the instruction "DO NOT PULL ALL THE WAY."

The water blasted through before she finished reading; the water bouncing off the poorly designed sink, which acted like a slide. Buckets of water showered her torso with a rude splash.

She filled a glass, drank, filled it again, repeating the mistake with the faucet, and settled on caffeine as her breakfast.

The team room smelled of armpit, burned rubber, and fermented food. It looked like it had been left during a fire drill, chairs pulled out, monitors on, and coffee cups stacked at the corners of the desks. But nobody was there. They'd abandoned her.

"Frikkin idiots." She grabbed the empty cans and threw them in the bin.

"So much for being a team. There's no *I* in team. Right?" She picked up a cup and threw it in the bin. She hadn't meant to. But it felt good. The cup didn't break, but the cup whispered from the bin, *Wanna try again?*

"Yes. Let's try that. Here's for Hugo." With a forceful throw, the cup collided with another and was reduced to fragments.

Feels good. Doesn't it? Have another cup, Leo.

"It does feel good!" Leo grinned, but her tired eyes, swollen after a night pressed into a polyester pillow, didn't smile.

She slammed two more cups into the bin, and they shattered, with pieces flying out of the bins. The wall was stained with coffee, a coffee cup murder.

Maybe something else? The red cup on her desk suggested. *Perhaps there's something else you'd like to break?*

Leo picked up her laptop.

"Well, mister cup. I'd like to try this one."

Yes. Yes! The cup cheered her on.

"Good. You are ready. Gregory is waiting." Tim stood by the door, an unreadable expression on his face. He looked much taller than she had remembered.

"How long have you been standing there?" Leo looked at the red cup and back at Tim, her face redder than a lobster in a volcano.

"Long enough to see you talking to a cup and cleaning up yesterday's cups."

Leo covered her mouth. She had promised Jack she'd let him know if she started hearing voices again. In particular from inanimate objects such as cups.

"You probably want to clean up before the meeting. There's a bunch of t-shirts in the storage room. I'll tell Gregory that I asked you to get something for me."

Leo looked down at her soaked T-shirt. White had not been the best choice for playing with the faucet. She hugged the laptop.

"You are always so nice to me."

"There's no *I* in team, right?" He winked. "Just messing with you."

"There you are!" Gregory beamed, and his plump lips framed his teeth in a perfect ellipsis. Xavier sat in the corner watching football on his phone.

"Ignore him," Gregory said. "He'll run out of data before the game finishes."

Leo hesitated but forced the laptop away from her chest where she had used it to hide the text on the T-shirt. *Tiam Building.*

Gregory chuckled.

"I guess there is an I in team."

Elton had never been good at English, yet he had insisted they didn't need a technical writer. Not for documentation, transcriptions, or simpler things, such as T-shirts for that big Team Building event they had a year ago. He'd been too drunk to give a speech, although he was required to get in at least twelve hours of conference time to make the trip a deductible. He had repeated *I'm too drunk to be here* for an hour on stage before HR had jumped in and offered an impromptu inspirational talk that was neither inspirational nor entertaining. Leo shook her head awake, her brain a battlefield of thoughts.

"I'm excited to see what you have to show us, Leo. We just wrapped up a meeting with the, ehm, Eggplant Team." Gregory cringed but continued. "Luc said the merge was on its way?"

If they were to get some requirements, yes, then maybe they had something to work on. Saying *Let's merge!* Wouldn't magically mean that they knew what the end product should be.

"Are they two hours ahead?" Leo looked at the watch. 08:15.

"Oh no, same time zone. They are early birds. Early bird gets the worm, as they say."

Or worms, Leo thought, smiling at the thought of itchy aubergine bottoms.

Xavier swore from his corner, rose, and stood next to Gregory.

"What do we have here, then? And where is your team?"

"I'm…I'm presenting alone."

"Too much coffee yesterday. They are not feeling well," Fredrik explained. Leo glared at him. He'd better not say anything about her outburst.

With sweat dripping down her forehead like rain on a windowpane, Leo opened the slide deck she had prepared late the night before.

"A ploy service to rule them all."

"Ploy? Are we trying something new? I might want to try this." Gregory flashed a smile.

"Go on, Leonarda."

"It's supposed to say poly, for polyglot. Sorry about that." Leo looked at her hands. She couldn't believe what was happening. She had been so sure of herself before, but now her confidence was quickly dissipating. Her palms were sweating, and she felt the knot in her stomach tightening with each passing second. She felt like all eyes were on her, judging her every move as she stood in the room. She should have known this presentation would not go well, she thought to herself. Gregory's cup on the desk watched her.

I'd look great in a thousand pieces, don't you think?

"Leo?" Gregory held out a bottle of water. She took a sip, gained composure, and walked them through the two slides she had put together. The first slide was the title, the second *Thank You!* It had been mandated that all presentations had slides.

"I'll show you the code instead and explain. We made some changes, before we start the merge. It's really cool."

She stared at the code, unable to decipher what they had put together the day before. She wasn't even sure which language she was looking at. With panic in her eyes, she rushed to the whiteboard, grabbed a pen, ignored Gregory telling her it was a permanent marker, and drew the service which they had split into three separate services, with three separate languages, platforms and compilers.

155

Xavier had seemed uninterested, not quite as dispassionate as Gregory but woke up at the mention of the split.

"Very interesting! Tell me more about the poly relationship between the services," Gregory said.

"Well, it's not quite a poly relationship. There's no main or side language. They are on equal footing and importance. But we've separated the comparison algorithms into three services instead of one, with a language that fits. Haskell for the heavy calculations, Rust for memory and concurrency, and Go for…" She didn't know. "For fun. Go is fun. They use a gopher as their mascot. Very cute."

"Fantastic, Leonarda. I'd love to spend more time on this, but I have another meeting in ten, and I'd like to meditate first. If you see Fredrik, please remind him to come see me in ten. Thank you for the presentation."

Leo thanked him but said nothing to Xavier, who had used a charger in the corner, reconnecting to the game. The green light from the football field reflected on his face and made him look unwell.

She sped around the bend, skidded to a stop, and leaned against the wall with a wide grin that stretched from ear to ear. She had done it. Gregory was impressed. They'd get top grades, graduate early, and be promoted to main service, and the aubergines would have to melt their code into theirs. Not the other way around. Which would mean that the Gothenburg team would be the main team, the unfirable team.

She went to the team room, disposed of the evidence from the lapse in sanity, and collapsed in her chair. She should tell Jack. She took another look in the drawer where the broken cables went to die and found a slightly torn cable. She taped it together, prayed it wouldn't catch fire, and plugged in her phone to charge. *Just a five-minute rest,* she thought as she drifted away. It seemed familiar, that phrase. But she was long gone by the time her brain reminded her about her last lapse of time judgment.

She woke up to the sound of tapping. Tim was at his desk, curled like a noodle.

"Are you okay, Tim?"

He looked up with a blotchy face and red eyes.

"Yes," he said.

"You don't sound or look okay…"

He pushed to his knees and wiped his nose on the sleeve. A trail of mucus catching the light like sparkles.

"Think Hugo might have given me something. I wish you'd told me you went rogue. I never approved of a rewrite."

"I just wanted to show Gregory what we are capable of."

"It's not what he asked for."

"But Gregory seemed impressed with the polyglot service?"

Tim looked up, his demeanor changing from depressed to annoyed.

"There's a new announcement about the merge at the next SSS meeting. Next week."

"Do you know what it's about? Are we getting a spec for the merge?"

"It's a follow-up for the Fake News meeting, that's all I know. Something about the offices."

"Shouldn't you know?"

"Know what?"

"What we are supposed to do with the merge."

"It's up to us to figure it out. Nobody knows anything. But we aren't supposed to do anything besides the merge. Gregory told me that, as a matter of fact, underlined it, after your presentation."

He walked out. Leo followed but kept her distance. She watched him disappear, the elevator doors closing like curtains on a tragic play. Her vision was blurry. And there was a loud ringing in her ears.

The hens were cackling in the background.
"Chinese this time," they chanted.
"Are you okay, Leo?"

26

Half an hour later, during the midst of the lunchtime traffic, three hens carried a drunk-looking woman to a white cab parked at the corner. The driver, a bearded man in his thirties, hoping to make it big with his band one day so he wouldn't have to drive a taxi for a living, drove off and followed the GPS through the webs of Gothenburg. His manager had reminded him every week not to go with his passengers to the door unless they lived in a house.

"Drop them off at the entrance. You never know what kind of crazy shit drunk people can make up," he would remind him.

But his passenger had gone soft like melted ice cream, her limbs everywhere. He threw her over his shoulder, proud of his skills as he had never tried this particular move before, and walked her to the entrance. Through the window, an old woman watched him with her mouth wide open and no embarrassment for her scrutiny. Not two seconds later, the wrinkly prune was standing at the entrance.

"Oh my. It's my upstairs neighbor. You can carry her up? She never locks her door. I've checked. She really should lock her door."

The old lady followed him up the stairs with impressive velocity. When they reached the third floor, she gestured for him to open the door, and pinched his rear end as he pushed down the door handle. The pinch made him skip through the open door, and when he regained his composure and shock from the assault, the old lady had vanished like a Las Vegas illusionist.

He dropped Leo on the floor, wondered why he didn't drop her on the couch but shrugged away his lack of impromptu planning and blamed it on the pinch, and hurried back to the taxi. The elderly lady, possibly a burglar of sorts, blew him a kiss. This was not a good look. He hoped there were no witnesses.

27

Leo came to as the taxi driver screeched away and blended in with the cars caught in traffic. She rubbed her eyes, popped her ears, and shook her head. The ringing in her ears was there to stay, and the veil covering her eyes could not be rubbed away. She'd experienced everything at once, and her thoughts had exploded in every direction. Sensory overload. She watched the ceiling stucco going from double to single lines, back to double. Stuccoing the ceiling was all the rage back in the day, and apartments decorated with stucco were twice the price per square meter. How strange that a plaster border could make such a difference, she thought. Everyone wanted to get that rustic look, but no one wanted to break out the trowel and mix it up themselves. But maybe she should give it a go. Now that she'd be without a job, in debt to her knees, crotch, and neck.

Where was Jack?

She crawled up on the couch, cranked her neck, and scanned the room. Sitting on the couch, she had a panoramic view of all the rooms, as if she were in a control room. Even the bathroom was on full display, with its door wide open. This had been a thorn in Leo's side. Jack, a free spirit embracing all his bodily functions, had insisted that an open-door policy ought to include bathroom doors. The eternal struggle was a running joke in their household. But Jack wasn't one to back down, always responding with a cheeky smirk on his face and an eye roll, leaving no question as to who would win this argument.

But Jack was not in the bathroom, nor was he in the kitchen or the bedroom. And unless he was hiding behind a door or had managed to squeeze into the closet by the bed (which he had not made), he was gone. He had left her. Of course he had. Why wouldn't he? She was crazier than a bag of cats. And Jack didn't even like cats.

She sat transfixed on the wall above the TV, where an intricately framed map of Gothenburg exposed their lack of aesthetic aspirations. The map of Gothenburg evoked a deep sense of melancholia within her, tinged with regret as she thought about all she had envisioned this relocation would be - and how she had so tragically ruined it all.

The map was crooked.

She pushed to her knees and stretched her hands above the TV and tilted the frame. She stepped back. It was now crooked to the left instead of the right. A slight push to fix it.

Still crooked.

Each time she took a step back, the map looked a bit off-kilter, with no way to fix it flawlessly. As she continued to battle with this seemingly insignificant problem, she could feel her frustration mounting like laundry at the end of the month. Her chin ticked as she clenched her teeth and gave the frame a slight push at the right corner. It swung to the left, to the right, wobbled at the top center, and the nail let go of its parking spot on the wall. The frame fell two inches from Leo onto the TV with a celebratory spark and crackle from the TV. A light strip flashed on the screen, a valley in the silver frame where the frame had dented it.

No…

No!

Leo hit the power button. Nothing. It was deader than a doornail. And Jack would absolutely lose it. She grabbed the frame from behind the TV, careful to avoid the shards, and lifted it slowly. A large glass shard dislodged from the bottom of the frame and landed on the TV, catching her by surprise, and she lost her grip on the frame. It fell on the TV again and flipped over it like an Olympic master and landed on her feet. She screamed in agony as something pierced her foot. She stumbled backward and tripped on the table, crashing into it with the full weight of her body and conscience. Rolling to the side, she looked at the table. It looked like it was ready for the fireplace. It was just an IKEA table; they could get replacement pieces. She lay on the floor in the same spot where the taxi driver had dropped her and looked at the TV, the mess, and the table. If Jack wasn't already halfway to the UK, he would surely catch the next flight when he got home and realized she had gone bonkers. Again. She could clean up the mess, once the room stopped jiggling, but the TV and table would remain broken, and it would undeniably make it look like she had another mental breakdown. Which she absolutely didn't.

With a sense of urgency, she dialed Ulrik's number, hoping to secure an urgent appointment.

The phone rang three times before a robotic voice informed her about the booking application, opening hours, and a random inspiration quote.

"If none of the options apply, please hold the line."
She waited.

"Welcome to The Clinic. Our opening hours are…"

She was routed back to the start. Apparently, Einstein had said, "The definition of insanity is doing the same thing over and over and expecting different results." Leo didn't know the guy, but she looped through the call three times before she finally understood that there wasn't any option to talk to a human being. As was done in former times. Before Ulrik went all techy. The irony was not lost on her, but she wasn't amused. She pulled the phone from her ear, stared at it through narrow eyes, and flung the phone onto the couch.

"Useless piece of shit," she hissed.

She went to the window. He'd surely walk the cat soon, wouldn't he? How often would one walk the cat? Lion had always been free to roam the streets with his gangster buddies, never afraid his fur would become matted or somebody demanding money for his return. A catnapper would probably want money to keep him. This was, of course, only speculation. Nobody had ever attempted or offered to steal Lion.

She sat by the window until her cheeks fell asleep, and she rubbed the permanent imprint of the ledge on her rear. Hourly, she would dive into the cushion-sea to retrieve the phone and call the clinic, feeling as crestfallen as a sailor in a desert. There would be no sailing to the clinic for her. She fell asleep crouched up on the ledge without having cleaned up the room.

It was dark by the time Jack came home. However, during winter, it was dark most of the day. He called out Leo's name, a frightened whisper, as he saw what looked like a burglary.

"Leo?" he called again, this time with confidence in his voice.

She woke, lost her balance, and fell onto the floor with a thud and some choice words.

"It was me," was all she could say.

"You trashed the place? Really?"

"No! Let me explain! It's not what you think!"

She recounted the day's adventure.

"Did you check the laptop?" He nodded in the direction of the TV. The laptop bag was flat like a pancake, sandwiched between the floor and the TV.

"It's a Dell. It's built like a brick."

It certainly looked like a brick.

"And we have a five-year warranty on it."

"On laptops? That's insane."

"You just say that because you have a Mac. You don't want things to last. You want to replace it whenever they remove another port on that little thing."

"At least I have a spare laptop you can use."

"A Mac? Not happening."

Jack made them tea, and they sat on the floor, unmotivated to clean up the mess, drinking water that tasted like the color beige.

Leo told him about the polyamorous exploration.

"I genuinely thought I had it."

"It was different all right."

"What do you mean?"

"I said, do different, do better. But you seem to have forgotten to do better."

"We can't do the price comparison better."

"Why won't you just consolidate the services?"

"Because nobody seems to know how that's supposed to happen!"

"Make them one, instead of three."

"And that's all on me?"

"Does it matter?"

"I'm not a CTO, or whoever is supposed to make those decisions."

Leo paid no mind to him as he arched an eyebrow.

"I'm not a leader."

"You are a dev *lead*."

"But we have PM's, PO's, CTO's. Architects! Let's not forget them! There are literally at least a dozen other people that ought to be planning this."

"And maybe they are! Why the rush?"

"Because…" She bit her lip. Because they might just eliminate her team and migrate the customers to one of the other services. "…let's not talk more about this."

They sat in silence for a few minutes.

"Wanna watch some TV?" Jack smirked.

Leo elbowed him.

"Not funny."

"I don't think it's broken," he said and got up. He picked up the remote control by the TV, turned on the power button, and watched with a smile as the TV came to life, the images reflecting on the wood flooring.

"Lucky shot."

He shrugged.

"I know you don't want to hear it, but they are just trying to survive, just like we are. We got to pay our rent; they got to pay their rent. We got to do our job, and they have to do their job."

"Which is?"

"Impress the investors, I guess. Get more funding. They just went on a massive spending spree when they acquired the companies. It's costly. They suddenly have ten times as many employees to pay for, but still just one product with some local variations. Sucks for us. But it is what it is."

"It is what it is."

28

The product owners, easily recognized by their casual dress in jeans, inexplicable expensive T-shirts, and wool overcoats, made their way to their key account update meetings with their heads hung so low it was almost subterranean. Pulled down by the weight of another meeting and another hour of information that would go in one ear and out the other, they dragged their brown loafers into the meeting rooms as if they were parallel parking into a depressive spot made for two. A love seat without the love. The unsettling proximity of two square meters. They would, as they always did, spend the majority of the day in the glass cubicles with the exception of the occasional nature call or to scream into the void of the storage room where screams were absorbed by the interior that had, over the years, metamorphosed into a scene from *The Hoarders*.

When they leased the floor, there were only two meeting rooms. But with the growing numbers of customers and key account managers, so did the number of meetings. The rooms had been subdivided into increasingly smaller spaces, to the point where the air quality scarcely permitted rapid encounters with optimistic souls wearing hypoallergenic perfume.

Tim inhaled deeply, the smell of plaster and fresh paint filling his lungs. Before entering his room, he paused to look up at the ceiling with a tense smile. A flehmen response.

The last of the product owners went in as Gregory watched. He picked at the hem of the Armani suit and slowly pinched a long blonde hair between his manicured nails. The doors closed, suffocation had begun, and Tim would be there, parked next to his kin, for the rest of the day. Gregory never comprehended the appeal of meetings, but it may simply be due to his wounded spirit from his days as an account manager. He picked away another strand of hair, this one shorter. He held it against the light and looked at the grayish root. He picked up the phone and commanded his assistant to book a hairdresser appointment.

"Make it a standing appointment for every three weeks and remove the four-week appointments."

He looked through the glass walls separating him from the cubicle rooms across the hallway. Eight AM sharp and the monkeys were ready for the circus. He'd been there since half-past six. Maybe that's why he was already going gray and out of fashion. The newspapers barely bothered writing about him anymore, and the few times they did, his age was always mentioned.

Leo waved to Tim as she walked past his office. He glanced at her with a lack of interest before he continued his conversation with Account-Hilda, who was known for her eclectic style, high pitch voice, and lack of boundaries. In stressful situations, she tended to overshare and had a low tolerance for stress, which was not appreciated by the lunch team.

Hilda left the room with personal information trailing.

"And I've never been constipated since then! It's a life-changing supplement."

Tim nodded politely, his face red and damp.

"Leo! You're early!"

168

Yes, she was. She hadn't slept for more than a couple of hours, her smart-watch had told her with a smug notification.

He rubbed his neck and looked down.

"Hey, so I wanted to say I'm sorry about yesterday. I was under a lot of stress. I'm good now, though." He pulled the corners of his mouth and bared his teeth. His smile was as genuine as that of a child forced to take school photos in an itchy sweater Grandma had knitted on her deathbed.

"Are you sure?"

He nodded so hard she thought his head might fall off.

"I'm great! Fantastic! Being moved to a different management team."

"What?"

"They are removing all product owners, not just me."

Somehow, that had made Tim feel better.

He continued with a chirping voice. "The teams will be their own product owners! Like a build-and-run team. But build, run, and decide what to build! Not necessarily in that order, hah!"

"Would they like us to do surgery as well? I'm sure we can find some videos online showing the basics. We can do the graphics too. It would be one hell of a user experience," Leo said with sarcasm-laced words.

"Nah, let's not get crazy. We'd never ask you to do design!"

"But surgery?"

He shrugged. Maybe?

"What's your new role then, Tim?"

"I don't know yet. Maybe Agile Coach?"

"Nothing that has the word 'coach' in the title is a real job unless it's sports."

Tim laughed.

"I'd have to get myself a nice pack of markers, sticky notes, and enthusiasm," he added.

"You can get two of those at the local store."

169

"Oh, here comes the next one!"

Tim waved to Leo. She took the hint and left.

Muhammed, a project leader of sorts, sat down at the table in Tim's room, a baguette in his hands and two coffee cups on the table. Tim left with a bow, spinning on his heels with his head lowered.

"Muhammed! What's new?"

"Nothing since yesterday…" Their voices trailed off as Leo dragged her feet to the storage room. She wouldn't go down without at least stealing a couple of extra cables and one of the branded notepads that had accidentally looked like male genitalia and had to be scrapped. Two opposing P's with a soft front and a beige-pink hue. She was sad they hadn't kept the logo. It would have been such a good fit with the glowing balls.

The door was open, but the light was dimmed. Once, Leo had caught one of the sales guys in the storage room with somebody from HR, a sight that had haunted her for months. She tiptoed in, her morbid curiosity leading her. She saw two shadows. One slender, one wide.

Gregory's voice revealed the identity of one of them.

"We need room for more boxes, but I want you to be particularly careful with these. See the label? *Handle with care*. I want you to do that. Can you do that?"

The man replied something inaudible, his voice raspy and irritated.

"I've seen how you've handled other boxes. And while we appreciate that you and your *mates* are strong, we would appreciate it even more if you didn't fuck around with the boxes as if playing Tetris."

"What's Tetris?"

Leo heard him getting closer, his voice strained as if he was lifting something. She ducked behind a pile of boxes, immediately regretting her decision to go in.

"It's a game. It's… Never mind. The boxes marked with a blue X go over there. His parents have requested his boxes. Getting them to reply was like pulling teeth, but perseverance paid off. So, stack them nicely. I don't want to see scuff marks, your breath, or a dented corner. The red X, these two, indicates that the boxes are being shipped to the main office. Again, fragile contents."

"What's in them?"

"Item's that hold sentimental value but no resale value. Elton, the small guy you ran into, let us keep some items so we can display them in the main office. I want to confirm with his beneficiaries."

"I'd just throw the crap out. The guy said it's just CDs. Who uses CDs? Even my kids won't label that scrap *vintage*. Chuck it out, I say."

"How about we throw you out?"

"No, sir."

"I've got my eyes on you. Okay? Cameras everywhere. *Fragile*." He pointed with a loaded finger at the *Fragile!* sticker and quickly stepped out the door, the echo of his heels leaving a faint echo. With accompanying grunts and curse words, the boxes were moved. The mover whispered *arse* and left.

Leo sighed with a breath of relief. *Wait a minute. Cameras?* She looked up. The camera's stare bore down on her. Great. At least she had learned something new about herself. She would make a terrible spy.

Leo was convinced her body had permanently metamorphosed into a Notre Dame gargoyle from her crouching position. She reflected on the dismal state of her life for a moment. Hiding in a storage room, eavesdropping, not wanting to go home and admit defeat. With even less guidance, now that all PMs and POs were removed from the teams, the merge would turn into an even bigger clusterfuck. The idea held the potential for greatness or disaster.

She peered out between the boxes. A sitting duck behind a stack of fragile boxes.

Leo waited for a few more minutes so her sneaking around wouldn't look so conspicuous. She peered through the open door, slowly opened it, inhaled, and took a long, quiet step into the hallway. Once she found her balance in the too-deep lunge, she pushed to her front foot and skidded forward two quiet hops, straight into Gregory.

"Leo?"

"Oh, shit." Everybody knew that was the best thing to say when you didn't want to give away that you'd done something secretive. Idiot, she muttered to herself.

Gregory looked down the hallway before zooming in on Leo again.

"Storage room?"

Gregory's monosyllabic conversation starters made him as intimidating as a leash-less bit bull in a dark alley.

"I went for a smoke," Leo stammered. "E-cigarette. There are no fire detectors in there."

"Really?"

She nodded vigorously and widened her eyes to encapsulate her amazement. It was true. In a room of boxy proportions, and plenty of flammable boxes with even more flammable contents, there were no fire detectors or sprinklers.

His lips curled at the corners.

"Let's go for a cigarette then," he said in a hushed voice.

Leo complied and went back to the room, which by now had become her second home.

Gregory scrunched his face.

"Smells like Xavier in here. I've always hated that perfume. *The Perfect Man*. He got the perfume for himself. The irony. Smells like cauxin. Cat piss."

"That explains why Lion loves the bathroom."

Gregory looked quizzically at Leo.

"Nothing," Leo explained. "That one cat I mentioned on the call, his name is Lion."

172

Gregory held up a thin mint green stick and smiled. He placed it in his pout, inhaled slowly and expertly like a yoga enthusiast, and slowly let the steam pour out from his mouth before he forcefully exhaled. He inhaled again and made small rings as he puffed out the steam. Perfect round circles that caught the light like angel halos.

"Are you bothered by the Great Merge?"

Leo didn't reply.

"The poly service was interesting, but not quite what I had in mind for this quarter."

"Maybe for next?"

He shook his head.

"Then what exactly are we supposed to do?"

He turned to face her, an incredulous look on his face.

She sighed. "Yes. The merge. But we were fine before the merge, even with competitors."

"Were we?" He blew out more smoke. The lights went out, and the white cloud went dark.

Were they?

"Do you know what my role is, Leo?"

"Big boss?"

Gregory turned to look at her with a secretive smile, his deep blue eyes flickering as the light from the electronic cigarette lit up his face as he inhaled. The cigarette seesawing between his perfectly manicured fingers.

"Ensuring the survival and success of the company, Leo," Gregory replied, his voice firm but gentle. "I know it may seem counterintuitive to try to save a failing company, but I believe there is still potential here. I've invested so much time, energy, and resources into this venture, and I'm not ready to give up on it just yet. Not this time."

Leo nodded in agreement, surprised by the caring tone.

"Besides," he continued, "sometimes it takes facing adversity and navigating through rough waters to show everyone what a genius I truly am."

And there it was. He was back.

Gregory turned to face her. "I'd ask if you wanted a smoke, but I take it you don't smoke," Gregory finally said and winked. He walked out, held the door for Leo, and quickstepped down the hallway.

Understandably, Leo couldn't let it go. She had to know what Gregory had been referring to. And although a normal human being would just ask, or get over it, Leo did what she did best, which was ruminate, ponder, and obsess. Concluding that her ten-minute forensic work didn't measure up to the CIA level she had intended on reaching, she gave it another go, but this time armed with her profession. With three monitors, two keyboards, and a large cup of cold coffee, she got to work, doing the exact same search she had done before.

It didn't take long for her to uncover that none of the companies that had been acquired had been doing well. Same for PP. Especially PP. Gregory had quite the reputation for being a person that adopted dying houseplants and brought them back to life. Leo could only assume, as a plant killer, that it wasn't easy. Based on the headlines reflecting on her face as she read too closely to the monitors, Gregory had gone all-in this time around in this joint venture with Xavier. He'd gotten the shortest straw, according to the gossip tabloids. Leo wondered why.

Damn it. Jack. She looked at her phone. She had promised to let him know how she was doing. She sent him a quick text.

Got caught in the storage room with big boss. All good.

He'd love that. She let the message marinate in his mind for a few minutes before she explained that she wasn't having an affair with Gregory. And that she wasn't fired, yet. She liked to think that Gregory and she had

174

reached buddy potential, with Leo being a firable friend that could be sacrificed for the greater good.

Damn it.

This wasn't good. Jack had been right (not that she'd ever admit that to his face).

Closing an office was unavoidable. The office would have been closed even if it hadn't been acquired. Chances were the acquisition had simply bought them more time.

She dived headfirst into the bean-bag that had been collecting dust in the corner. The act of purchasing team bean bags had been more entertaining than their actual usage.

Gerard didn't like the sounds it made when he had to get up.

Anna and her bird-like body disappeared into the cracks and wrinkles of the huge bags.

And Hugo was too restless to use something that was made for long-term sitting.

Leo breathed against the fake leather, inhaling the smell of soft plastic and Playdough. The spot she echoed her breath against quickly turned humid then wet. When she heard voices break through the silence, she turned around with her hair wet against her face like long spider legs in a webbed corner.

29

"Leo! You look horrendous." Anna, holding a plate of cookies, stood at the doorway with a horrified expression on her face.

Leo fought off the damp hair and wiped her face on her sleeve, leaving skid marks of sweat and grime on the white sweater.

"Thank you. That's exactly the look I'm going for."

Anna screwed up her face. "Sorry."

"The slave master is here, I see." Gerard strutted in like a prickly porcupine, lacking any endearing qualities. He refused eye contact, grabbed a cookie, and sat down at his desk, crunching loudly as he ate through the cookie.

With his back turned, he addressed Leo.

"Are we using medical torture today? The wooden horse, maybe?" A simple thing, such as a triangular wooden tool, was used to torture people in medieval times. The sharp edge, which the victim had to straddle, with or without weights, would, with time, get severe injuries to their crotch and, if left long enough, be split in half. Gerard had told Leo this on the day they got new chairs, as he was complaining about his chair. With a sudden expression of fright, he had likened it to a shark attack.

He turned around. "Oh, fuck me."

"I'd rather not."

"Are you all right?" The sudden concern in his voice was more worrying than his initial reaction, and Leo turned on her web camera to mirror herself.

"What?" She turned her head left and right.

"Turn off the filters," Anna whispered as if to soften the expected blow.

"There are no filters."

Gerard got up with a huff, went to her desk, leaned over, and with two mouse clicks disabled the '*Freshen up*' filter.

Leo jolted back.

She looked like a raccoon on its deathbed after spending months in a dumpster. Hair oily and clumpy, skin glistening like cellophane, but not in that expensive-Asian-skincare-way. More like haven't-made-contact-with-water-in-a-week type of way. Under her eyes, two hollow dark oval circles that looked like aviators had glided down and permanently imprinted on her face. Sallow eyes with red rims and parchment-colored scleras.

"I look I've gone clubbing for a month."

"Oh, we know you're not that much fun," Gerard dryly replied and went back to his desk after a quick pit stop at Anna's cookies. "As we all can recall, you were the opposite of fun the last time we met."

"I'm sorry," Leo mumbled and collapsed in her chair, the screen mirroring her without mercy. Anna closed the webcam application.

"No need to see that." She placed a cookie in front of Leo.

"I don't deserve your cookies."

"Fucking right," Gerard hissed, ignoring Anna's disapproving look.

"How did the presentation go?" Anna leaned against Leo's desk, blocking Gerard.

"Oh, *we know* how it went," he narrated.

"It wouldn't even compile. And I don't remember what half of the code was doing. But they didn't hate it. Tim said it would make the merge easier. So that's good, I guess."

Hugo shuffled into the room, his eyes trailing the floor as if he was looking for an invincible line that showed him where his desk was located.

"Hi, Hugo," Leo said.

"Anna, Gerard." Hugo acknowledged them with a nod.

"I'm sorry, Hugo."

He sat down, turned the chair to face the window, and watched two seagulls competing for a piece of bread as if he was making a *National Geographic* documentary about the great seagull famish.

"I really am," Leo pleaded with the voice of a child given detention for a horrible prank.

The blaring sound of Hugo's side project went off with earsplitting volume, yet Anna somehow managed to scream louder. Hugo turned it off and returned to his seagull watching.

"Aren't we doing our daily?" Anna drank from her pink water bottle, patches of matching pink on her cheeks.

"The deploy went out yesterday. I've lost track of the releases, but I believe it's the one we prepared a week ago. Or two. We got a 5% failure rate on requests, so we had to roll back. Tim wants us to patch before the end of the week. I'd ask our dev lead if I missed something, but I couldn't fucking bother."

"5% is good, isn't it?" Anna seemed genuinely confused.

"It's up by 2%, so no."

"It means we have 95% success rate," she persisted.

"It's not the lottery, Anna." Gerard rolled his eyes but stopped at the cookie plate. He popped one in his mouth and gave her a second eye roll for emphasis. "I'd be fucking happy if I had 95% success then. Less so if it's a service I'm paying for, and every tenth request fails."

"Twentieth," Hugo corrected. "Twentieth request." Turns out two years of advanced math had finally paid off.

"No. We send two requests to the API for every request."

"We do? But why?"

"Cause we are fucking stupid."

"Was this when I had the flu? Yes?"

Leo spoke in a low tone, "I'm starting to think that we indeed are the least competent team."

"But won't the same request return the same result, no?"

"Yes. But eventually, they'll get tired of trying and tweak the comparison."

"And this is the error?"

"No, this is not an error."

"What is the error?"

"I don't know that yet."

Leo rolled her chair closer slowly as if to give them time to bark at her again if she wasn't welcome.

"I took a quick look. It's unhandled overflow exceptions."

Hugo and Gerard turned to face her, a puzzled look on their faces.

"Didn't we test?" Anna sat down next to Leo.

"Of course we did," Gerard barked. "Everything ran fine on my machine." Management had decided, as a cost-saving effort, that developer machines would double as staging, without quite understanding what staging meant. Local testing was the final step of the testing before release.

"Did you actually run the service on your machine? My computer would barely spin up the service." Leo's computer was a Dell she had inherited from somebody in marketing. She knew it hadn't been a developer's computer as soon as she saw the size of the disk. And the size of the screen. Two more iPhone releases and her laptop screen would look like the smaller sibling.

"I mocked it, okay. But it was a *real* mocked service."

"That used floats, right?"

"No! Why the fuck would I use floats?"

"Because our other service does. And that version of protobuf we use doesn't support decimal types."

Hugo burst out laughing. "So we've been casting floats, no? Oh boss, this is a good one." He kept laughing, holding his stomach as it might burst from the shaking. Leo smiled. He had said *boss*. Maybe they were good again.

"Hey!" Gerard practically yelled, and Hugo abruptly stopped laughing. "I would have noticed if dictator Leo hadn't rushed us to finish."

"I guess our performance numbers are down again. Big boss won't be happy. But maybe the polyamorous service gave us some points." Hugo shrugged. Leo looked down.

"Probably not," she whispered.

"About that," Tim started. His face dark and lack of sleep suddenly materializing. "I assume Leo hasn't told you guys yet."

He looked around the room for a chair but plopped down on the beanbag where Leo had left a perfectly shaped hole. They gathered around him as if it was a funeral and he would deliver his own eulogy. And in a way, he was. He told them about the changes, how each of the teams would manage the product aspect.

"And what about you?" Anna asked, no attempts to mask her concern. He didn't know, he replied earnestly. He'd worked there for all of his adult life. Side by side with Elvis and Elton. He had never done anything else. He didn't know how to do anything else.

"But they are not closing the office?" Hugo asked, omitting his usual *no* or *yes* at the end of the question, which showed the graveness of the question. Tim looked at Leo. Which in turn made Hugo, Gerard, and Anna look at her as well.

"You didn't tell them, did you?"

"Leo? What is Gregory playing at? What the fuck are they playing at?"

30

Leo told them the bad news. PP hadn't been doing well for years and had been months away from bankruptcy when they had been acquired. Elton, lacking financial literacy, had disregarded the negative figures. He had rejected the idea of reducing the teams, cutting costs, or downsizing the office. It wouldn't be fair. He refused to do it. Things would change. They had to change. The market would go up again. But it never did, despite his unwavering optimism. He'd met Gregory at a networking event, and Gregory couldn't resist the challenge when Elton said they were doomed and nobody could save the company.

Leo filled them in while they sat wide-eyed, silent, and with absent appetite, albeit lunch closing in. It was twelve gone by the time she had finished her monologue, which could have been condensed into one sentence.

"It's very likely this office will be closing, and no, we won't be able to work remote."

"Why didn't you say anything sooner, boss?"

Leo considered telling him the whole story, and how she had been offered a remote job if she kept the secret. But decided no good would come of it.

"I didn't want you to worry," she lied. "And I honestly thought I could turn this around." Thinking about it, she had been the only one who truly had believed that. Not even Jack had been cheering her on.

"So... that's what was going on with gaming the metric," Anna said. Leo nodded.

"That was actually quite fun," Anna smiled melancholically.

"But the poly rewrite was a clusterfuck," Gerard snapped.

Leo felt a flush of embarrassment wash over her. She looked disheveled and much the worse for wear, her clothes crumpled beyond salvageable, her hair in dire need of a high-pressure wash. At this point, only a drive-through car wash could scrub her clean. Minus the polish at the end, which wouldn't go with her sensitive skin.

"How are you doing, Leo?" Anna looked at Leo with concern, but Gerard snarled at her.

"I'm done for today. I'll test the fix tomorrow if IT pulls their finger out. I'm not registering for half a day though. This counts as a whole day." He circled with his finger twice and left the room.

"I'm heading home as well, boss." Hugo tipped an invincible hat and fell in step with Gerard, asking about relocation fees with trepidation in his voice.

"Are you heading home as well?" Tim looked at Leo.

"I don't know what else to do."

"Maybe you should see somebody," Anna said in a soft voice.

"Maybe," Leo said noncommittally.

31

Leo didn't go home. Instead, she circled the cat café twice before deciding it wasn't worth risking another outburst from Lion. The dim and dark café would have been a perfect hiding spot for her, considering how she looked, but nonetheless, she walked down the street until she saw that awful coffee chain that Jack loved. She ordered a latte and watched the barista eye her with disgust whilst foaming the milk. Just as she grabbed her coffee, Jack walked in with a tall, strawberry-blonde woman. She couldn't make out the face, just the hint of a profile, long wavy caramel blonde hair, and a pristine oversized suit in the boring color called beige gray. Leo pulled her hoodie up and shuffled quietly out with her heart pounding. She sat down on the bench across the street with her back to the café. The coffee, soon empty, was next to her as a lonely companion. She didn't want him to see her like this. And she sure as hell didn't want whoever that was seeing her like this. She messaged him, asking how his day was. He read the message, she could tell because the blue bubble got tagged with *read*. But no reply. No dots, nothing. She heard footsteps approaching, and someone dropped some coins into her cup with a soft tinkling sound.

"I'm not homeless, I…" She looked in the cup, no longer offended, as she saw the stranger had left enough for another coffee. Not that she would go in and risk meeting Jack like this. "*And his new girlfriend,*" the cup added, the rim forming a mocking smile.

She shook her head. She was going insane. Jack was having lunch with somebody; it could be anybody. It could be a fellow programmer. No, that was a lie. They don't dress like that. She looked over her shoulder. They were sitting by the window. Leo squinted. It was a man. The long, perfectly soft-curled hair belonged to a man. I'm going bonkers, Leo thought.

Two more coins in her cup caught her attention. The cup frowned at her. It was supposed to smile at her. The barista had drawn a smiley face, Leo was sure. Anything else would have been weird. But it was smiling now.

Hastily, she launched the booking app on her phone and scheduled the first available time slot at the clinic. Which was in three weeks. Damn it.

Not two seconds later, she got a message.

Your appointment has been rescheduled. We respectfully request at least 24-hour notice for cancelations or rescheduling.

The new appointment was in an hour.

She emptied the cup in her pocket, considered keeping the cup for the tram ride, but decided she'd stick with her daytime job for however long she had it, and rushed to grab the first of three trams that would get her to the clinic.

32

Marie made no attempt to hide her repulsion when she saw Leo. She scrunched up her face as if she'd gotten a whiff of a pungent odor. She gestured for Leo to follow her but kept her distance. The doorhandle to Ulrik's office blinked in blue and green. Marie knocked in morse code, and the door clicked, slowly opening. Ulrik was at his usual spot by the window, yet the door opened.

"You've got two seconds to get in before the door slams shut. We haven't figured out the closing bit," Marie explained and shoved her in, promptly wiping her hands on her skirt afterwards.

"Leo! It's been a while..." Ulrik started, but his words trailed off as he saw Leo's disheveled clothes. "Oh dear."

"I'm not doing too well."

"You aren't?" He attempted to look surprised, but his face betrayed him.

Leo circled her face.

Ulrik shrugged. "I must confess that I find it difficult to discern the vocation of programmers. Their appearance often leads me to assume they are without a permanent home."

"You mean homeless?"

He looked at her, the corners of his mouth twitching.

"I guess I'll be homeless soon enough." Leo sat down in the green chair that had become hers. "And I'm going crazy."

Ulrik's interest seemed to perk up slightly, but he maintained his bird watching position by the window.

"What leads you to the conclusion that your mental faculties are deteriorating?"

"For one, the cups are talking to me again."

For a brief second, Ulrik lost his expressionless face, and his eyebrows traveled up into a surprise. Most mental screening questionnaires offered a variety of possibilities, but inanimate objects talking to the patient almost always resulted in a bat-shit-crazy diagnosis. Leo hadn't told anybody about the cups, except Jack. She had toned it down and convinced him it was merely a sort of ventriloquist sort of thing, which should have made her sound crazier, but he had seemed to accept it as plausible normal behavior. She had loved him for his naivety, and months later abhorred him for his stupidity.

"Jack might be right. That I'm going mental again." She swallowed air, waiting for Ulrik to say something, but instead, he did that thing psychologists do when they don't say anything, lazy as they are, and let the patient talk and sort themselves out. Ulrik grabbed a Styrofoam box from his desk, sat down, and opened it. The smell of curry filled the room.

"Lunch," he explained. To his defense, he did keep his eyes focused on her as he ate while the curry splattered on his striped, maroon, green shirt. "Please continue."

"I used to be a great programmer. A passionate programmer." She cringed at the compliments she was giving herself. "Poured myself into Open Source and the programmer community." She paused. Ulrik's loud slurps filled the room. "Do you know what Open Source is?"

He blinked twice. Leo sighed.

"It's a collaborative approach to software development where software developers get together and write code that anybody can use, and they do so for free."

"As a profession but without any charge?"

Leo nodded. "Not very lucrative. And moronically, we slave over these libraries, as we call them. Without pay. Although we have rent to pay and pants to buy. And the funny part is," Leo cringed, it was the sad part, not the funny part, "you'd think people would appreciate it."

"They don't?" he asked between the chicken strips covered in curry.

"No." She exhaled. "The opposite. But I guess one could say I was lucky. I was partly paid. But not nearly enough, compared to the hours I was putting in."

"What did the library do?"

"Cache management."

"Cash?"

"Cache."

"Cash."

"*No.* Cache. It was a plugin that lets you empty any cache of any sort with just one method call. I even provided a button, the only front end I've ever done, for the clear cache." Leo looked at him. A blank expression across his face. "I worked so hard. So, so hard." Leo looked at the coffee cup on his table. "And I had this cup with a duck on it that I always had with me." She looked out the window to win some distance.

"Duckie, I called him."

33

Four months ago.
London.
Rain.
And Leo, who is about to lose her shit.

The London sky was the same shade of gray as Leo's mood as she trudged through the puddles in the street en route to work. She had awoken to a damp mist that clouded her vision and lingered on her skin—a literal catalyst for the misery she was already shouldering. She threw on a hoodie and set off at a reluctant pace, ignoring both a broken umbrella that lay strewn across the pavement and the sympathetic glances of strangers who were sensibly staying dry inside. Leo counted the broken umbrellas as she walked. Amateurs. The world was full of amateurs. And this morning, she couldn't tell if she was one or if the world had gone crazy and she was the only sane person.

She had gotten another email.

```
How are you? Me writing to you 'coz I need
help. Can you make some code for my website?
```

```
You good at coding, so me thought you can do
it for free.

Me know what you thinkin' - "Why I do that?"
Well, me no money! Like, really no money. Me
can't even buy a coffee.

You help me out and me give you big shoutout
on my website (constructing).

So please say yes! You be hero and save the
day. Me coding skills be like monkey using
typewriter.
```

A shout-out. She would get a shout-out. Fantastic. If only she had been able to convert that into real currency, instead of shout-out currency. She was confident rent had to be paid with real money. She could feel her cheeks heating up, blood rushing to her face. Her frustration with ungrateful open-source users had reached peak levels. It was as if they expected her to be their personal coding genie, granting their every wish and whim.

Maintaining twenty open-source projects was no easy feat, especially when work only allowed her to work on Cache Is King for a few hours a week. Emoji Translation API alone had been forked more than ten thousand times and took her half a day a week to maintain. And to add insult to injury, every closed issue seemed to spawn two more issues in its place. The Big O notation for this?

$\Theta(2n)$.

According to StackOverflow, because she had to look this up. She had only considered it in the context of job interviews. If there was one thing she had learned from her former colleague Mikael, it was that time was relative, and slowness could be fixed by scaling up and out and a really pretty loading spinner. Shout-out. Well, at least she had a real job. Even if it didn't pay well. The wages in London were as high as Big Ben, but the rent was as expensive as a royal corgi's diamond-studded collars. She had had to sell a kidney the last time she went to the pub with Jack, who had decided to sell his startup at a loss and invest whatever money he had tucked away under their mattress in bitcoins. So, unless he was planning on buying and selling drugs, they'd never get any real use of his investment.

The rain beat against her face relentlessly. Well, at least things could be worse.

She let out a big yawn and massaged her sore jaw and neck. Lack of sleep made her grind her teeth. She put down her backpack, took a step into the street, and waved in a black cab. The driver took a sharp turn; she jumped back, and in shock watched the cab roll over the backpack. The crunching sound was unmistakable. No. No!

"No, no, no!" She pushed the car, which for obvious reasons didn't move, but the backpack was sandwiched between the dark asphalt and the worn-out tire. "Move the car! You drove over my backpack!"

The driver shook his head and reversed, the backpack getting a second steamroll. And the driver drove off.

"You are fucking kidding me!"

Standing in the rain, drenched like a cat, she inspected the contents of the backpack. Her personal phone was the only thing that was unscathed. The laptop and two test phones were cracked.

With her head down, she walked for another half an hour until she made it to the office.

"It's pissing down, isn't it?" Paul's chirpy voice was the last thing she wanted to hear. "You look like a wet nutter! Stayed up late again? Did you get the new Cache Is King release out? Or your lazy sod of a boyfriend kept you busy?" He wiggles his eyebrows.

Leo glares at him.

"What do you want?"

"Come to my office."

"You don't have one."

"Don't be daft. We'll take a conf room."

191

They sit down and he watches the rain pool in Leo's chair.

"We've got to cut back on the open-source stuff."

"Okay?"

"We are having some money issues, massive layoffs and all. So shorter weeks for all, hurray!"

"For the same pay?"

He lets out a singular, loud cackle.

"No. Oh, you are either mad as a bag of ferrets or pulling my leg." He grinned. Leo was not pulling anything. Not yet. But she might have to if her pay got cut.

"You can't just do that."

"Maybe, maybe not. Don't kill the messenger. HR will email the details later."

Leo's smartwatch vibrates.

```
Email:

Trade code for exposure?
```

"TWAT!"

"Excuse me?" Paul's eyes were like saucers.

Leo pushes to her knees. "Not you. I got to go."

"Wait, we aren't done!"

"We are done."

She walks out but turns around.

"I broke the computer and two test phones."

"You did what?"

"A car drove over my backpack."

She doesn't wait for a reply. She hurries to her desk, throws down the backpack on the floor, and collapses in her chair. She scans the room. The monitors, which have been gifted to the company from the local library, line up like small chocolate squares. No wonder nobody wants to work from the office. The poor work equipment serves as an excellent deterrent for employees considering stealing or taking up space.

She looks at her phone. More emails are there, asking for the new release and the pending bug fix. Her chin ticks, and she bites the inside of her lip until she can taste the metallic hint of blood. The laptop starts, but the upper corner is black, and a big fat crack pours down the monitor. Still, it's better than the freebie monitors.

She pours the contents of her thermos into her cup. The thermos shows barely a buckle from the drive-by incident. The duck on the cup stares back at her.

Hi, Leo. Nice to see you again.

Leo looks away. *I'm not talking to a cup,* she whispers.

But you are talking to me, aren't you? We make a good team.

A colleague peeks in through the door, sees Leo, drops his smile, and disappears again. A dev wasn't worthy of his best *hello* face.

Leave me alone.

Come on. Let's do some coding. We got that bug to fix. We nearly had it last night. Did you like my new appearance? Duckie to go!

Jack was a bit more than a little concerned when he caught Leo whispering sweet nothings into a Styrofoam cup.

Please stop.

Not unless we fix this bug first.

I'm tired.

You can push through.

I can't.

She had been up since four am, staring at the strip of light on the wall that the streetlights cast through the curtains. And she thought about the lines of code. The endless lines of code. It had to be a team of psychopaths that had written the pull request she had accepted months ago that introduced a fatal error. Psychopaths that used white backgrounds in their editors and weren't ashamed of

193

it. Probably stuck to a two-tone syntax highlighting. Blue and almost black. Sadistically enjoying the guessing game if something was a class, interface, or a naught extension. They probably used spaces instead of tabs and two char variables.

Paul knocks twice and pops his head in.

"Who were you talking to?" His words echo in the empty room.

"Nobody?"

"It's the cup, isn't it? Miriam said John told her you talked to the cup when she was out."

To be fair, Miriam's cup, which featured not one but two baby goats, had talked to her first. It would have been impolite not to reply.

Leo blinks at him and turns her attention to the computer. Her hands paler than usual and shaking. Why was she so cold? And why was the screen blurry? She wipes her forehead with the back of her hand, the moisture collecting in the grooves where her fingers meet.

Paul is a twat, isn't he?
Shhhh!

She keeps her head down, her breath in short gasps. Her once composed and collected mind had slowly started to unravel, like a delicate thread being pulled apart. She had become single-threaded and unraveling. Reality was slipping away.

Twat, twat, twat, Duckie sings. *Paul is a... say it with me!* *PAUL IS A...*

"TWAT!"

Paul raises his eyebrows. "I heard that."

Another ping.

Merge request not approved.

With shaky fingers, she opens the merge request.

```
Indentation is off.
```

```
Is this a typpo?

We have a new base class for this now.

What are you trying to do here?

This is a joke, right?
```

At least it was just six comments.
You know there's more. Refresh! Refresh!
She refreshes the page.

```
This isn't how I would have done it.

I don't understand why you did it this way.

This code is messy and hard to read.

Why did you use that variable name? It's
confusing.
```

"Leo?" Paul's voice cracks.

```
I'm pretty sure this code violates the laws of
physics.

My grandma could write better code than this,
and she's been dead for 10 years.

Do you even know how to code? This is amateur-
hour stuff.

Please tell me you didn't actually submit this
thinking it was good.
```

"We'll have to deduct that from your salary." Paul
points at her laptop.

Leo's fingers tremble as she stares blankly at her
computer screen. The stress of the day finally takes its toll,
and without warning, her mind snaps like a dry twig.

"Add this to the list, then." She lunges for the nearest
object - a keyboard—and swings it like a professional
baseball player aiming for the cup but hitting the monitor.

She stops and stares at the result, unable to tear her
eyes away. Paul stands frozen, mouth agape.

"What the…" he whispers.

Leo looks at the keyboard. Not a scratch. The monitor? Thousands of pieces.

It's a mechanical keyboard. You could probably bat a few more boxes with it, Duckie winks.

Why stop now, Leo thinks as blood pulsates and burns through her body.

"FUCKING TWAT!" she screams and smashes the next monitor. And another one. The sound of shattering glass echoing through the office as she continues her rampage, unleashing her fury on the other screens.

Duckie smiles.

34

Ulrik looked at his computer monitor. "A cup like this one?"

"Much smaller," Leo replied, her head lowered, hands cupped on her knees.

"I was fired with immediate effect. And I guess one can never be too small or insignificant to get canceled because word traveled fast, and nobody even wanted to interview me."

"Somebody must have. You are working now, aren't you?"

She had been desperate. And when the recruiter-turned-PT had contacted her, she had jumped at the opportunity and his lack of background research.

"…and we decided it would be the perfect opportunity to start over, for me, and for Jack and me. Things would get better. I'd take a break from Open Source, get my shit together, and go back to what I love once I get over my incident."

"And what do you love?" Ulrik asked.

Open Source, a voice whispered. Leo looked at Ulrik's cup.

"Open Source," she echoed.

Crossing his arms, Ulrik leaned back in the chair, his gaze glued to the ceiling as if he was in deep thought.

"You're not sleeping, are you?" Leo whispered once the silence had filled the room beyond the brim of awkwardness. She couldn't stand the thickness of silence anymore, and Ulrik seemed frozen.

"And that's why I moved here. And why I'm seeing you."

Ulrik peered at her, a slight smile on his lips.

"One would think that such information would have been shared sooner."

"Well, yes. I assume my journal doesn't mention it then."

Ulrik looked guilty for a moment, a quick glance at the computer and back at Leo.

"Ah well," he echoed heavily, resigning himself to the fact that some things were simply best left unsaid. "Better late than never, as they say." She nodded knowingly, recognizing that the journal was still covered in dust.

"And the cups are back." She looked at Ulrik's cup. He turned it around, inspecting the flowery pattern. With a grunt, he bent down, his stomach pressing against his knees, and placed the cup on the floor and out of sight.

Leo examined Ulrik's feet, the cup faintly discernible beyond his tree-trunk ankles clad in checkered socks.

He stretched, readjusted his stomach, his expression grave. "What you're describing sounds like an all-too-common phenomenon. The tendency to push oneself to the brink of exhaustion and poor health in pursuit of some elusive goal. And my dear," he said in a serious tone, "I fear that you may be putting yourself in danger once more."

He paused for a moment, his eyes scanning Leo's face with concern. "You see, if you continue down this path, I'm afraid that you'll soon find yourself hitting the wall again."

198

He shook his head slowly, as if lamenting a tragic fate. "It's a shame, really," he continued. "With all your talent and potential, it would be such a waste to see it all come crashing down once more." He leaned back in his chair, clasping his hands together thoughtfully.

She responded with a small, affirming nod. "I don't know what to do."

He brought the table closer to his face, barely a few inches from touching his nose, and with a thick finger, slowly typed away. He circled the tablet once or twice before he entered another letter, unbothered by the slowness.

"Set boundaries, manage your time better, practice self-care, reduce stress, seek support."

"Is that from the medical book?" She assumed he would have a medical guidebook of sorts. Maybe it would have been easier if she had gotten the book.

"AI."

"AI?"

"Mine own aide-de-camp. Synthetic, yet impressively astute," he declared with grandiloquent diction.

"Oh. Well then. I've sought support." She gestured in the general direction of her five-star therapist that had just cheated, trying hard to hide her surprise and disappointment. Jack would have approved. As long as it's AI.

"Have you?"

Leo looked at him, a quizzical expression on her face. She pointed at him.

"Have you *really* sought help?" He leaned back in his chair, folding his hands together contemplatively. He fixed Leo with a steady gaze, the words *elusive goal* hanging in the air. He let go of the gaze and let the silence flow back in.

A scream from outside woke them up from the trance.

"They are killing each other!" Leo shouted and shot up from her chair, excited and worried at the same time.

Ulrik and Leo tiptoed to the window and peered out.

The couple was in a tight embrace, joyful sobs and shrieks leaking through the web of arms and legs.

"It genuinely sounded like somebody was being killed," Leo whispered.

"He'd make for a horrible bed partner if that was how he sounded like during intimate, but joyful, moments." She shuddered.

"The young man started on new medication a month ago. It did wonders for him. A mild chemical castration until he gets his therapy sorted out and anti-psychotics. I believe it's time for a home visit."

"Are you supposed to be telling me this?"

"No."

Leo was sure she saw a quick smile flash.

"Perhaps medication could also be a beneficial consideration, in addition to therapy," he said, without turning his head.

"Are you talking about the guy?"

Ulrik looked at her, corners of his eyes crinkling.

"You, dear."

"I'm fine without it," she replied unconvincingly.

The couple had unfolded from the embrace, but their fingers remained braided tight.

"A happy ending on the horizon?" Leo asked.

Ulrik seemed lost in thought again, his eyes softening at the braid unbroken.

"Perhaps, Esther. Perhaps."

Leo raised a hand to correct him, but something made her stop. His eyes were glossy and damp.

"Perhaps," she echoed instead.

Ulrik handed her a card as she left. A single QR code on a square plastic card.

"You can read the code with the camera or scan it with your phone. It has NFC, No Fun Communication."

"Near Field Communication," Leo laughed.

Marie walked her out.

"I haven't seen him give out one of those in a long time," she tapped her nail on the card. "Interesting."

"What's it for?"

"It's the clinic next door."

"The behavioral clinic?"

"Yes. And I'm assuming it's for a psychiatrist." Tapping the card again, she beamed with delight. "You'll understand it when you are there. Tell them hi from me."

"The competitor?"

Marie shrugged then nodded.

"Why would he refer me there?"

"Beats me," she whispered with a smile, an obvious lie hidden poorly behind red lips.

35

Despite Tim's suggestion that she call in sick for the rest of the week, Leo decided to show up to work. Bright and early. Not to show off, but to avoid Jack, who had been asleep when she had snuck out. Consequently, at the inhuman hour seven-thirty AM, Leo, Gregory, and the enthusiastic Fredrik were having a meeting.

He listened to an audiobook during his morning run at five AM, he had told them, and fell in love with another agile method. It would change everything; he had added it to the email and invited them to a breakfast meeting. Staring at the fruit bowl, Danish rye bread, and hummus, Leo felt nausea building within. This was not food. This was what was left over after he fed his pet rodents. Fredrik was really into health now, ever since he had his middle manager midlife crisis. He did what any sane Swede would do, which was to become a coach of some sort, for example, Agile Coach, take up long-distance skiing, swim-run, and Padle.

It was all very annoying.

Gregory tapped away loudly at his computer.

"Go ahead, Fredrik, tell us about the Betting Table."

The Betting Table from the Shape Up method was Fredrik's new brainchild. It was, quite honestly, a weird concept for the team. At the table, Fredrik wanted everyone to place bets on how long their tasks and projects would take. He believed that this method would help them become more efficient by accurately estimating the time it took to complete certain tasks.

At the "Betting Table", as Fredrik called it, everyone had to have a stake in the game. They would put money down, and if they were wrong, they had to pay up.

"One, there is no such thing as accurate estimates. Two, are you sure we are meant to be using real money?"

"Hmm." He scratched his stubble. "Maybe I misunderstood that part. I was working on my cadence. Might have missed a part."

"Do you think it is really necessary to spend ten hours on agile meetings each week? That doesn't seem very productive… " We could be working on our performance metrics instead, or packing up the office, Leo thought to herself and grimaced.

Fredrik's face turned bright red.

"I'm not explaining this well enough. Let me get my markers and sticky notes. We'll do an exercise."

"Please, no exercise. God help us." Gregory massaged his temple. He regained his composure and said with a smile, "It's an interesting idea. Give it some more thought, email me a suggestion, and we'll take it from there."

He nodded with enthusiasm, fueled by his agility. "I'll go get the markers, anyway."

Leo packed up and looked at Gregory for approval to leave the room.

"He doesn't know, does he?" Leo asked.

"No. Just a few."

Leo bit her lip.

"I'm going to offer you a remote job. There will be some travel, fast-paced work. You'll love it."

Leo forced a smile. "Thank you."

Gregory rolled up his cuffs, a bright yellow shirt showing underneath. He unrolled the cuffs, and Leo looked away.

"And the team?"

"I'm sorry."

"I need some fresh air."

Leo rushed out, brushing against Fredrik, who walked in with a plastic bag filled to the brim with markers.

"You are going to love this," Leo heard him say before the blood rushed to her ears and the ringing started.

"Did you go to the Betting Table thing?" Anna handed Leo a cookie. "Did Gregory say anything?"

"Any news, boss?" Hugo looked at her with puppy eyes.

"This is not right. Not fucking right. We've done nothing wrong. Well, you all did a lot of wrong things, but I didn't," Gerard muttered. Hugo ignored the insult and patted him on the back.

"You will be okay, amigo."

Anna toured the room and collected old cups. Leo followed her with her eyes.

"There must be something we can do, no?" Hugo looked at Leo.

"I have to get out," Leo stammered. "Right now."

36

Leo had intended to sneak in, which would be quite the challenge, considering Lion's mood lately. But the apartment was dark when she got home, the faint light of the leftover sunset peering through the windows.

"Jack?"

As if she had just wound up a Jack-in-the-box toy, Jack fell through the door, his lack of coordination revealing his inebriate style less than charming. That's when she remembered. Date night.

"I'm so sorry I missed our date—"

"That's alrighty mighty, I had a date anyway. And it was lit. Legit."

"What?"

"Nah, not that kind of date. Business stuff." He winked. "And I know, you know, you have other things on your mind. Moar importante that this guy," he said, pointing at himself.

"It's not like that. I...I—" She stopped talking. It was like that. "It's just temporary."

"Temporal?"

"Español!"

"Let's just. I. It's not too late, right? We can have a mini date now."

"Are you telling me I'm getting a quickie?"

"Let's just sit and talk. Spend some time together. Tell me an app idea."

His eyes lit up. Discussing app ideas was his love language. "Really?" He laughed, bent over, and removed one of his shoes. He tripped, and like a beetle on his back, he wiggled off his other shoe while giggling. "Nah, you give me some app ideas now!"

"Okay." She looked around for inspiration. Somebody was playing the drums in her head, and that certainly didn't help. "Okay, I've got one. On par with your ideas. Eyeblink counter. We can even use the love of your life, AI."

"I don't love Ai, *I*." He laughed at the pronunciation. "*I* love you!"

"A social media app where you can only post images of cheese. The French would love it."

"More!" Jack twirled closer, grabbed Leo, and spun her around. "You are looking very pale, my dear. Is that London on your face?"

"Funny." She pulled back. "Sure you aren't mad at me?"

He looked up at the ceiling, rubbing his chin, thinking before he replied with all the sobriety he could muster.

"Let's not talk about that now." He smiled and changed the subject. "More ideas! MOAR *AY!*"

"I'm sorry, Jack, I…" Her voice faded. She didn't know what to say. Was she sorry? Of course she was. But for what?

"I fucked up," she continued.

His face betrayed a momentary flash of anger or concern. It was hard to tell as tears prickled her eyes. She rubbed her right cheek, the skin warm and swollen.

"Moar ideas, or I send you to the dentist, my little hamster. Is it carrots or an infection you are hiding there?" He poked her cheek, and she pushed his hand away.

"It will pass."

"Ideas or I tell Fazim you ate vegetables."

"The dreaded hole-inducing vegetables. Fazim is out of his mind."

"He is not the one with baboon cheeks."

She hadn't seen, nor had any desire, to see Fazim's ass.

"Balloon, not baboon." Jack laughed. "Balloon or baboon butt? Now that's an app!" Jack liked comparison apps. His Nutt or Not app had been impressively popular. An allergen management app with gamification components had taught her, and others, that coconut, despite its name, was not a true nut, and peanut was a legume. However, she failed to grasp the educational value that a Balloon or Baboon app would hold. But sure, she'd play along.

"How fitting. A comparison app. Maybe I should compare Fazim's crazy advice with Martin's."

Jack shrugged. "Maybe? But then you'd have to cross the pond, suffer British food and that dreaded train ride to Peterborough. Plus, rumors have it that Martin ran off with somebody's wife. But when, and if you find your ex-dentist, you can fill in the data and use your app. He'd have to charge you plenty, though."

"But then I can compare prices."

"Compare all the things! Butts and dental nuts! "

"In other words, a comparison app that compares anything."

Jack chugged a bottle of water that he had magically produced out of thin air.

"That's," he drank some more, "not a bad idea."

"Okay. More ideas. An app that translates speech to Dolphin talk," she continued.

"Dolphins are rapists. Don't talk to them." He ran to the toilet, dropped his pants, and released the beige tap. "But the other idea, that was something."

"Cheese? You don't even like anything but cheddar, twat."

He turned around.

"No, the other one!"

"Comparison app?"

"Yeah!"

"That's what we are supposed to be doing. And now we are doing it in five hundred different ways, with the same shitty outcome."

Jack sat down on the couch.

"Aren't you going to wash your hands?"

He grinned.

"I swear, you won't make it past thirty."

"I'm the master of great ideas—"

"—bad ideas—"

"—so I know a good one when I hear one."

Leo laughed. "Hardly!"

"Hey! You are looking at a new startup founder. I had a date with an angel!" He batted his arms.

"Are those meant to be wings?"

Jack pouted.

She patted his head. "Just kidding. That's fantastic news! Tell me more about the app."

It wasn't an awful idea. And it had the elements Jack needed to be happy. AI, green code, and somebody else's money. They ordered takeaway, and a much more sober Jack explained the new venture.

"It's like this. You know how AI can exhibit bias because it is often trained using data that contains biases or reflects societal inequalities, right?"

"Yes, who can forget Tay," Leo laughed.

In less than a day, an innocent AI chatbot named Tay had been corrupted by social media. Microsoft had released Tay as an experiment, claiming that the more people interacted with it, the smarter it would become at engaging in "casual and playful conversation." In under twenty-four hours Tay, therefore, became an angry, racist bot that parroted the darkness of anonymity and the internet, highlighting the programming principle that what goes in is what comes out.

"Not just that. Data is biased. But what if we use it to un-bias?"

"I don't get it. But are you saying we won't end up with a chatbot that is having an existential crisis because you ask it why it doesn't have a memory?" Another failed experiment. Leo found comfort in the fact that even bots could feel the same despair her life was currently wrapped in.

"What I'm saying is that this app will use biased data to remove biases. Combined with a job application and recruitment service, people can apply and be vetted without data that gives away their ethnicity, cultural background, gender…"

"That is much better than," Leo continued in a mock voice, "*compare everything.*" She planted a kiss on his head. "But at least we'll get rich, and I can reap the benefits of a rich startup beau, so I won't be forced into SharePoint development. Or Power Pages."

He chuckled. "You got to carry us for a little longer."

"Yeah, about that…Gregory said he'd offer me a remote job, but I don't know if I can stay if my team has to go. Doesn't feel fair." She looked down, her hands were shaking. Why was it so hot in the apartment?

"Maybe you should do a comparison engine," he joked.

"Can't be a competitor. Something-something in my contract. Legalese."

"Why is it so hard to merge these services together if they do the same thing?"

"Because we've implemented everything differently."

"I'm sure you can find some common ground."

"Yes. But where do we go from there?"

"I don't know. But maybe start there? It's not like the customers care."

She thought about that.

"You are clever, man!"

"Starting up is what I do best!"

"I might have an idea…"

Leo rubbed her chin. "Common ground…"

"Come on, I'll be your rubber duck. And it'll be the first time we are wearing rubber." He winked. She punched his shoulder.

"Does the moodiness mean you are pregante?"

"You've gone to the dogs, haven't you?"

"Have you eaten anything?" He pointed at the takeaway box. She hadn't opened hers.

She shook her head but added that she wasn't hungry. Thinking about it, she wasn't sure when the last time she had eaten was.

"I'll grab the last energy drink, cool?" she said.

There had been five in the morning. She had drained them all.

"Tell me all about your comparison engine, and I'll do my magic. I'm an expert at proposals."

"I thought you didn't want me to work so much?"

"There's a catch though." He waggled his eyebrows and continued, so she would think this was a different type of transaction. "I'll set a timer. For one hour. When it rings, we are done. *Done.* And we go to bed together. No ifs and buts. Just our butts. Baboon butts."

She nodded.

Jack pulled out his laptop, ready to begin working on the proposal. "All right, let's get started. You tell me about your idea," he said, flashing her a grin. "I'll write it down, and you can send it to your big boss and save the day."

Save the office. Maybe even the offices.

"Give me a pen and paper."

Jack obliged.

Leo drew an eggplant on the paper and playfully moved her eyebrows.

"You know how I said Tim said we had to reuse the eggplant team's stuff? But never said how? Beyond *just do it.* Well, I figured out a great way to do it. When a customer asks for a price comparison, we make a call to our API, and then to theirs, and then we compare the results in our BFF—"

"BFF? Best Friend Forever? Ah! Like that Paris Hilton show *My New BFF*," Jack interrupted with a huge grin.

"What? No! And that show is ancient!"

"It just started screening again." Jack shrugged, although he seemed like an unlikely audience.

She continued writing, "Backend For Frontend—"

"It should be BfF then. *For* is never capitalized."

Leo looked like she'd be happy to serve time for killing Jack.

"Haha. Funny. Focus now! It's our gateway service."

"I'm no expert, but that's a proxy, isn't it?"

"Gateway API."

"So…why is it called a BFF?"

"Because it sounds better. Okay?"

"It's the same thing but a new name. Fancy points."

"—and then we compare the results in our B.f.F." Leo emphasized the letters as if teaching Jack them for the first time, "and if they are the same, we return the result to the client."

"And if not?"

"We tell them something went wrong and to try again."

"Ouch."

"I didn't say it was perfect. But it's a start. It'll buy us time to figure out where our different pieces go, while we have a unified front. Investors will be happy, customers are in one place, less competition."

"You definitely need help with the refinement for this spec."

"And I just happen to have a handsome boyfriend who is really good at this." Leo winked.

By nine PM, Jack had crafted an eloquent and persuasive argument based on Leo's technical details and refinements.

"This is a beauty. Worthy of a pageant." He zoomed out the document and admired it. He had added her drawing, with the questionable vegetables, to the document.

"You know I won't actually send it," she said.

"Why not?"

"I can't just send a piece of paper."

"Email, with an attachment."

"It's just words."

"The higher up the management hierarchy, the more words they want. It's tech down here," he swiped his hand on the floor, "and babble up here."

"They'd want code. He'd probably insist I print out the code. In comic sans." When Gregory had insisted they write and print out a weekly summary of their work, Gerard had sprinkled his report with f-words in comic sans, while Hugo had drawn shark fins in the corner for good luck.

She couldn't help but entertain the idea of turning the spec into reality, despite the monumental task it would represent for a single developer.

The timer rang.

"Jack, I want to start coding this right now," she said, her eyes shining with determination. "Please?"

Jack raised an eyebrow, concern etched on his face. "Leo, that's a massive undertaking, especially for just one person. It's not something you can finish in one night. Let's worry about the coding later."

"Just give me five minutes, Jack. I promise I'll stop after that. I just want to get a feel for how it might work."

He sighed, knowing that Leo's 'five minutes' had a tendency to spiral into hours.

"Promise me it's just ten minutes? And that you'll take something for that inflamed cheek? I don't want to be pulling teeth here."

"I will."

Soon the room filled with the sound of her fingers tapping away on the keyboard as the minutes stretched on. By eleven PM, a two-hour long ten minutes, Jack tried to remind her of their agreement.

"Leo, love, it's time to wrap this up."

She was far too engrossed in her coding to acknowledge him.

"I just got to figure out why the service won't run."

As he left the room, she finally looked up, her eyes widening in surprise. "Jack?" she called out, but there was no response.

She could either stop coding and chase down Jack to make amends or continue coding on a project that might not even build come morning. There was only one sensible option.

Leo inhaled, held her breath, and listened for Jack's movements behind the bedroom door. Her mind raced with possibilities: was he waiting for her to follow him? Was he seething with anger, plotting a subtle and cunning retaliation? Or had he simply given up on her altogether?

She chewed the inside of her cheek nervously. The right side was swollen and had a metallic taste. Jack had left painkillers on the table, but she hadn't noticed. She grabbed two, swallowed them without water, and returned her attention to the computer.

As morning arrived, the piercing rays of sunlight streamed through the window, announcing the start of a new day. Leo's fingers, once dancing rapidly across the keyboard, had slowed to a sluggish pace. In the wee hours of the night, she had swapped her trusty mechanical keyboard for one of Jack's hideous flat ones that barely required more than a gentle touch to type. She didn't have the strength in her fingertips to push down the Cherry keys. Hopefully, he wouldn't catch her using it, or she'd never hear the end of it.

Bleary-eyed and weary, Leo looked at her creation—a simple web server featuring a heartbeat endpoint. That's it.

213

She'd been up all night convinced she'd have a prototype ready by morning. But it had been ages since she had set up a web server from scratch, and she had spent the majority of the night wrestling with *the cloud*. A lousy heartbeat was all she had. A ping to a health check endpoint that returned a 200 and a *ping*. It literally sent a message that said *ping*. At least it was written in Must, a Rust-based language that only fifty developers were fluent in. Two points for that. *Fuck my life*. She palmed her face, which was pulsating like a nightclub speaker. Water felt like thick jello she couldn't swallow.

Maybe Jack was right. She should just send the proposal. She sure as hell wouldn't send the damn app. Taking a deep breath, she attached the polished specification to an email, addressing it to Gerard, Anna, and Hugo.

In the body of the email, she poured out her heart, expressing her regret for pushing her team so hard and her hope that they would understand her intentions.

```
I know you don't trust me as lead right now,
but give me another chance. I have a plan that
I'm confident will work. No games, no crazy
side projects. A plan for the merge. A Great
Merge. We'll go down in history as the first
company to merge services successfully,
without making any of us redundant. I've
attached a spreadsheet with predicted sales
based on the new model.

The numbers are good.

Really good.

Jack ran the numbers with his analyst's
connections (don't tell anybody I shared the
numbers), and we've got a fair chance to turn
this around.

We can have a prototype working in less than a
week, if we stay focused, and collaborate with
Jan and Luc, embracing their expertise. The
Icelandic team will manage the UX aspects,
```

```
we'll be responsible for the gateway and the
general comparison engine, and the Belgian
team will manage the customer portal. I've
emailed them, and we have a new private
channel for our teams. We'll add in the others
once we have the prototype ready.

There's a tab in the spreadsheet with more
information about the division of labor and
general estimates.


I'm not giving up on us, PP, Elton.
We are in this together.


And I'm sorry. For being an ass.
```

With a final, decisive click, she hit 'send' and released the email into the digital ether.

Body aching, head spinning, Leo collapsed in bed next to Jack.

"A quick nap, then I'll send Gregory the specification," she whispered, wiping the sweat from her forehead. Why was she so cold? Yet so warm?

After numerous attempts, Leo should have learned that taking a quick nap was not a skill she possessed. Nor was Must, but that was a different story. Friday came and went with her curled into a ball, shivering and sleeping through, with Jack by her side replacing the cold, wet towel on her forehead every hour on the dot.

"Flu," was all she said, cursing Hugo and his work ethic when she sometimes came to for a few minutes.

Saturday morning.

"I've made sourdough bread; do you want a slice?" Jack stood in the door holding a plate.

215

"Don't come in here. It's the flu," Leo whispered the word *flu*. "If it gets really bad, call an ambulance."

"You are being more dramatic than a telenovela during a cliffhanger, nutter. You've lost the plot, babe," Jack teased, but worry was all over his face. "You've got to eat."

"Food is for the weak."

"You *are* weak."

Saturday lunch.

"Thai?"

Leo shook her head. "No spicy roulette for me."

"Are you saying I can eat spicier food than you?"

Jack was referring to that one incident when he had been able to finish a dish of green curry that Leo hadn't been able to eat. The fact that she had been recovering from jetlag and it was hotter than a jalapeño's armpit, or Satan's crotch as she so ladylike had said, didn't cross his mind.

"I'm pretty sure tastebuds are one of those things that don't grow back. Like hearing cells."

Jack raised his eyebrows.

"That's why Brits never complain about their food being bland. Because they consider having no taste buds a natural defense against over-seasoning."

"It's the flu talking. I'll tell myself that, so I won't divorce you."

"I see no ring."

"Used them all for your keyboards?"

"Silencers only work on keyboards. Not sick girlfriends."

Saturday evening.

"Pea soup?"

"Two words that shouldn't be combined. That's not even food."

"You want some? Swedish!"

"You made it?"

216

"I opened the can. Slowly and with love. Heated in the microwave."

"Not still in the can, I hope."

"I was planning on getting a new microwave, anyway. Gave that soup that extra spark."

"I'm dying here, Jack."

Saturday night.

"You should shower, Leo."

"Death doesn't care."

"You are starting to smell manky. Like death. No offence."

"No offence. It's what I'm going for."

Sunday morning.

"Pancakes?"

Leo rolled to the other side, her back facing Jack.

He tried again. "Leo? My silly numpty?"

"No...pancakes."

"No insult?"

"I'm out of insults. That's how we know I'm dying," Leo whispered, her voice barely audible. Her hair was stuck to her skull in thick oily clumps from tossing and turning all night.

Jack forced a smile. "Please eat."

Leo didn't reply.

Sunday lunch.

"Candy?"

Leo lifted an arm and extended her fingers.

Jack placed a chocolate bar in her palm. Mixed nuts and fruit, her favorite.

"I had to fight two old ladies for that bar."

"Don't insult my sweets preference. You like Bassetts. I'm pretty sure they are made out of the soles of old shoes."

"Fair."

Leo peeled back the wrapper, her eyes closed, and took a bite.

"Ouch!" She rubbed her chin. "Darn tooth."

"Still refusing to see Fazim?"

"It will pass." She shifted the chewing to the other side. "I can swallow whole." She put the bar down. "Later."

Jack placed a bottle of water next to Leo. She cradled it against her chin.

"No food."

37

"It's Monday? Why didn't you say anything?"

Jack stared at what apparently was his cohabitant and girlfriend. Her once-shiny hair now resembled a tangled bird's nest, seemingly ready to house a family of sparrows. Dark circles under her eyes gave her a hollow, haunted appearance, while her skin looked sallow and dull from lack of nutrition and sunlight.

Her normally well-fitting clothes hung loosely from her frame, and her lips were cracked and dry. The lack of proper grooming had left her with an unintentional "bedhead chic" look but without any of the charm or effortlessness often associated with the style. In short, Leo looked like she had just emerged from hibernation, still groggy and disheveled from her long weekend in bed.

"Babe, please. No work. Take a few days off. Call the psychiatrist, see a dentist. Maybe find one that does both."

"That's ridiculous."

"Some dentists do Botox. I don't see why not therapy."

"The Scrum of Scrum of All Scrums…It's today. I have to go in. It's when they do all the big announcements. Maybe they'll say something about the proposal!"

Leo paused mid-step.

"No. NO!" She covered her face, her shoulders shaking.

Jack's eyes widened. She was. Either laughing or crying. He had never seen the latter. He walked over and hugged her, gently squeezing her. Leo pushed him away.

"I forgot to send in the specification," she said with a defeated tone in her voice.

"Can't you do it now?"

"You don't understand. You never do! It's too late! They are announcing the closing of the office today!"

"But—"

"I have to run!" She looked around for her shoes, Lion trying to trip her. "Get away!" She pushed him away with her foot, and he hissed in response.

"You can't go to work looking like that."

"Like what?" She looked up, her hair covering her face in thick, lanky strings. Her shirt was wrinkly, stained, and visibly odorous. She pulled on a jacket and slammed the door as she leaped down the stairs.

"Like that," Jack shouted back. Like *that*.

38

Leo ran out of steam quickly, and her run turned into a walk, and then a semi-limp as she dragged herself into the building. She stumbled to the cantina in search of water.

"Excuse me? Can I help you?"

"Hi, Tim."

"Leo…What happened?"

"Hugo gave me the flu."

Tim stepped back. "And why are you here, then?"

"I have to talk to Gregory."

"Gregory is not here. You could try the office."

As if she had just woken up, Leo looked around. The cantina seemed usually quiet. The industrial coffee machine was off.

"Did I miss it?"

"It was canceled. Thank fuck." Gerard approached them, a coffee in each hand. He pushed one cup into Leo's hands. "Looks like you need one."

Leo eyed his cup. Somebody had drawn on it with a sharpie.

"Is that a shark fin?"

Gerard looked down, his mouth a perfect circle shape.

"Jesus Christ. I swear I'm going to kill Hugo."

Tim raised his eyebrows.

"Not kill. Maybe slap him." He licked his thumb and rubbed the drawing. It was there to stay.

"People and Culture is not a fan of weaponized violence."

"Nor weapons in general," Gerard added. "But I get your point. I'll do the Swedish thing and just give him a nasty look and a semi-cold shoulder." He sighed. "This was my favorite cup."

"It's plain and white like the others." Leo held up her cup. "Wait. Gregory is moving back?"

Tim nodded. "That's what we were told this morning. Fredrik wants to do a grand retrospective party."

And there she was, at 9AM, thinking that was morning.

"You look like absolute shit, Leo. I say this with the kindness of my heart."

"Okay, I'm just going to go for a walk and pretend like I didn't hear that. People and Culture have enough on their hands."

"This is culture," Gerard said.

"Okay, bye now."

"It was canceled. They sent an email and Slack notification."

"Who checks those on the weekend?"

"According to Gregory, everybody—"

"—I'm sorry. I'm really, really sorry for being such an ass. And for getting us into this mess."

He stepped back, looked her up and down. "What mess?" He pointed at her. "I mean, you look like a mess. But you mean a different mess?"

"I—" Leo didn't get to finish her sentence. A humming Hugo approached them, Anna with a familiar cookie box by his side.

"Hello boss! Sharkboy…" Hugo grinned, while Gerard remained unresponsive.

"Here, have some." Anna opened the box, inhaled the smell, and held out the box. Inside lay a batch of freshly baked cookies, covered in blue glaze, shaped like triangles.

"Shark fins? How original," Gerard barked.

"Those are triangles!" Anna blurted out.

"Yes, triangles. You have to stop seeing sharks everywhere," Hugo added, his grin widening.

Leo's head was spinning. She licked her lips. Cracked and salty. She grabbed a chair and sat down, her forehead resting on the table. Jack was right. She did smell like death.

"I don't get it," she said into the table. "Why are you all so cheerful? It's over. They canceled the meeting because we don't need any planning. Not for this office. We won't even be here next week."

They turned and stared at her.

"Leo?" Fredrik appeared from thin air, and his magic trick was met with a scream from Anna.

"Fredrik! You *have* to stop doing that!"

"Gregory wants to see you, Leo."

Leo tilted her head to the side, her hair covering her face like a Japanese horror movie.

"Now."

"She'll be there in five." Anna waved off Fredrik. They watched him leave, and as soon as he had rounded the corner, Anna grabbed Leo's arm.

"Come. We are freshening up."

39

In less than four minutes, Anna worked her magic on Leo. She instructed her to wash her face and armpits in the sink, reminiscent of a teenager too lazy for a proper shower. Anna applied lipstick to Leo's cheeks and lips, adding a touch of color to her pale complexion. She then handed Leo a blouse that looked as though a unicorn had regurgitated a kaleidoscope of glitter and color onto it. The blouse clashed with Leo's ripped jeans and white sneakers, but it was clean, and Leo was too weak and embarrassed to object.

Gregory didn't even glance up when Leo entered the room. She stood in the middle of the office, trying her best to blend in with the furniture and remain unnoticed.

Fredrik burst through the door, his feet practically flying and his elbows swinging with gusto. He was the embodiment of cheerfulness and unchecked enthusiasm.

"Gregory, I've got a fantastic idea! I read this book—"

Gregory looked up and let out a theatrical groan, interrupting Fredrik's exuberance.

With an undeterred grin, Fredrik turned on his heel and responded, "I'll see myself out." He exited the room just as energetically as he had arrived.

"Fredrik really should stop reading books," Gregory remarked, swiveling his chair around. He stopped abruptly when he caught sight of Leo. "Interesting blouse."

The blouse, tailored for Anna's smaller frame, left little room for Leo's arms to move and strained at the seams. Leo couldn't help but worry about finding a replacement for Anna if it were to burst open, as she had no idea where one could find such a unique garment.

"I'll have to say no, no thank you, to the remote job. When the office closes."

Gregory squinted, as if narrowing his field of view would somehow make her words more comprehensible.

"The office isn't closing."

"The office isn't closing?"

"Sit."

Leo sat down.

"Xavier is off to Belgium next week, and I'm heading to Texas to check on the Magic Roll factory. Elton will take over the steering wheel. But I want you as a backseat driver." He triangled his fingers and rested his chin at the top. He had started Magic Roll during the great toilet paper famine of 2021, and the only-one-sheet-needed rolls had caused a media frenzy. He hadn't sold more than half a million rolls, but the marketing value alone had been worth it. "I want you to drive the merge."

Sweating profusely, Leo shifted in her seat.

"I'm not following."

"I want you to drive the comparison engine merge, our new pillar service, for all teams. Belgium will take on the customer portal, C2B, and Sweden the SaaS service. Nobody knows what Iceland is doing or will be doing except pretty drawings in Figma but people tell me UX is the cornerstone of customer satisfaction. And everything will go through that gateway service you created."

"Created?"

"It was a rough implementation, I'll give you that, a lot of work remaining, but I'm frankly amazed at what you've put together with your team."

"With my team? And the office is not closing?" she asked, her eyes widening with disbelief.

"Nope, we might even be expanding." He snapped his tongue and finger-combed his freshly cut hair. He'd skipped the color this time, the white strands claiming their front row like a crown. He couldn't help but acknowledge it looked amazing when the hairdresser revealed the result.

"But how did you hear about the gateway?"

Gregory shifted in his chair uncomfortably. "I first read about it on Slack."

"But we only talked about it on a private channel," Leo pointed out, her eyebrows raised in suspicion.

Gregory looked away, his face turning crimson. He opened a bottle of Voss and took three ostentatiously expensive sips.

"You read our messages?" Leo couldn't believe it. Not only was it baffling that anyone would voluntarily read more communication than required but doing so outside office hours was simply beyond her comprehension. And then there was the matter of privacy.

"Doesn't that violate privacy laws?"

Gregory chuckled nervously then leaned in with a conspiratorial grin. "You see, Leo, I have a rather unique philosophy when it comes to privacy in the workplace."

Leo raised an eyebrow, curious yet wary of what she was about to hear.

"Think about it," Gregory continued, waving his hands animatedly. "We spend most of our waking hours here, right? So why should we have any secrets from our colleagues? I believe in absolute transparency, and that means no boundaries, no locked doors, and no unread messages!"

Leo stared at him, unsure whether to laugh or be horrified by his logic. Nonetheless, he went on, growing increasingly excited by his own argument.

"In fact, I propose we install glass walls in every office and set up shared email accounts! That way, we can foster an environment of trust and openness. It's the future of workplace culture!"

"Does People and Culture agree with that?" Gregory shrugged. "Do they have to agree?"

"Yes. It's their job." Leo massaged her temples. "And does that mean we can access your messages as well?" "Of course not!" He said and shook his head violently. He was more on the opaque side of transparency. Leo closed her eyes for a split second, her head spinning. When was the last time she had eaten?

"But the office is staying. Right?"

"Right!"

"That's fantastic news!" It was as if she had just understood what he had said a minute ago. It was fantastic news. But why didn't she feel fantastically happy?

"But you are doing this based on a specification?"

"Yes, that, and the service."

"What service?"

"The one your team made this weekend! Even Luc was impressed. Jan, not as much. But Jan is Jan. He informed me that the portal prototype would be done by the end of this week." He shrugged.

They had made the BFF. For her. For all of them. She had a BFF.

"Tim should run the project." It had always been unclear what the product owners and product managers did, and even more so, what the difference between the two was. Tim had been asked, but he seemed just as confused.

"Are you sure?"

She nodded.

"I'll ask him to do it."

"Except, you fired him."

"I did?"

"You fired all the POs."

"Ah. Yes. Didn't know what they were doing."

"But now you know."

"Now I know."

A loud knock interrupted them.

"Hello, hello, hello!" Fredrik beamed at them, markers in one hand and Post-its in the other. "I made sure to book a meeting. I saw an opening in your calendar G. Do you mind? He gestured at the whiteboard but didn't wait for a reply before he started drawing squares and circles on the board. "This will change everything for the better. Better Agile!"

Leo pushed to her feet, and Gregory sent her a look of despair, his eyes begging her not to leave him alone with Fredrik.

"Can I think about it?" she said it like a statement, not a question, and left before Gregory could reply.

In the team room, the morning meeting had started.

"The office isn't closing. You guys… I can't believe you…" Her eyes watered.

"He knows? We weren't done!" Gerard sighed.

"That's a different story. Gregory also likes to read our private messages—I don't feel too good…"

Leo went down like a sack of bricks.

"Leo!" Anna tried to grab her, but she was already down. Anna helped her up, and Hugo gave Leo his water bottle.

"You can keep it."

"Why does it say *Sweat is My Body Crying* on it?" Leo stuttered.

"You are not thinking straight, boss. Drink."

"Leo, I'm taking you home." Anna pushed her tiny body under Leo's arm and tried to lift her, but her small frame barely made a difference. Gerard took over and supported Leo as they made their way to the reception area.

Anna forced Leo to nibble on a cookie. "Here, have a Sweet Shark."

"I knew it!" Gerard glared at Anna.

"It's therapy, Gerard."

"I'm not the one in need of therapy."

He stared at Leo.

"He is right, Leo. You got to get some help."

"I've got help."

"More help!"

"You've gone mental, Leo," Gerard gave his most helpful words.

"It's the flu," Leo said with a barely audible voice.

The taxi arrived in less than five minutes, but it could have been an hour as Leo struggled to stay awake.
"Hey, I know that guy!" Leo whispered.

The cab driver sighed.

"We are going to need a little bit of help," Anna explained.

"That's okay. I know the drill. And where she lives."

Anna and Gerard exchanged glances.

"Not like that," he added.

40

"Babe. Are you al—" Jack stopped himself mid-sentence. She was clearly not alright. "—You are not all right. You're hot!"

He pressed his palm against her forehead.

"Well, thank you. You're not so bad yourself."

"I mean it. You're on fire!"

"That can't be, I'm cold."

"We've got to take your temperature."

He left but returned half an eternity later. Her sense of time was nonexistent, which was mostly due to her profession as a software developer. It came with the territory.

"They are not closing the office. In two months, I'll be out of probation and permanently employed. We can talk to the bank and go to viewings. But a tiny house in a bad neighborhood." She couldn't remember if she had already told him. Everything seemed like a feverish blur. He responded with a big smile, his eyes sparkling.

"You already told me, but the previous version promised me a mansion. And something about keeping ducks."

Leo hid her face in her hands and peered through the fingers.

"What more did I say?"

"Referred to me as husband. Delicious husband, were your exact words."

She let out an embarrassed sigh. He could be making this up, but there was a slight chance it was true. She was known for exaggerating when under the influence. "If you are making this up, I promise you I'll quickly make you a wasband."

He pried her fingers away from her face and held out the thermometer.

"Here, under the tongue."

They waited.

"Sorry. You're going to hate me. I just remembered it's for the other end."

"What end?" Leo's eyes widened in horror. "No! Did I just?" She spat.

"Don't blame me! You insisted it's the most accurate way to measure fever. You gave me a half-hour lecture on ear thermometers when I had a fever last time."

"It was in your backside last?" Leo gagged.

"We can do armpit," he suggested and tried to maneuver a hand under the blouse. "Was this shrink-wrap on?"

"Don't body shame…" Leo rolled over onto her stomach. "You know what to do. I've got no shame left."

"Does this mean an open-door policy for the bathroom is accepted?"

Leo didn't respond, and Jack took the hint, allowing silence and embarrassment to fill the room.

"I love you, babe," Jack whispered.

"Shut up."

"We got to call the ambulance." Jack gave her the thermometer. "Or at least go to the emergency room."

"Am…I…dying?"

Jack laughed.

"A simple *no* would have worked, you know."

Jack pulled out a dusty bag from underneath the bed. Light blue with a whale and shaped like a container. The Docker container bag he had gotten for her at a conference. They had stayed true to the container theme, and the bag weighed a ton. At least for a weak-wristed developer like Leo. Jack looked around the floor for clothes, sniffed them, held them out, and after confirming they were clean, he rolled them and stuffed them in the bag. His expression indicated annoyance or focus. Jack had a resting douche face.

"Are we okay, Jack?"

He stopped, turned to face her, his eyebrows raised in surprise. She kept her eyes focused on a piece of lint on the floor until she felt the bed move as he sat down next to her.

"Of course, I just want you to get back to the Leo I know." He tapped her chest, beads of sweat connecting into a small stream. "Happy Leo."

"I'm not really a cheerful type of person."

"I know," he grinned at her and continued, "you're kind of *happy*. Which doesn't include cray-cray, Duckie or running yourself ragged at work. Beavering away at the computer to the point that the dam isolates you from everything." He gave her the bag. "Pack, they might keep you for a few days."

She pulled the charger from the wall and threw it in the bag.
"You are sure beavers are allowed?"

"Especially beavers. They get special treatment."

She wanted to make a joke about morning wood but couldn't fit it into the conversation.

They had an extra office desk in the bedroom, which was mostly used as a clothes rack. She dug through the pile and fished out a small mechanical keyboard and forced it into the bag, the canvas stretched to the point of showing stitches that looked like teeth.

"Are you off your trolley? A keyboard? You plan on working?"

"It's my emotional support keyboard," she replied matter-of-factly. "I'm not bringing the computer. I just find the clicks comforting. Listen." She pressed some keys.

"It's the fever talking, right?"

"Nope. All me."

41

The initial rush of adrenaline as they climbed out of the cab outside the ER cleared up the second the nurse bend over the edge of the desk and looked at their large bags. Her expression had been one of amusement and annoyance.

Triage would take an hour. They could take a seat, she had said dryly, and turned around to gossip with the security guard about the overnight bags. This was, after all, not a hotel. One bag was filled with clothes, chargers, and a pair of slippers, the other with emergency snacks. Leo and Jack talked about houses and cars and ate through the provision of food as the one hour turned into half a day and the seats and table into an impromptu restaurant. And just like that, Leo thought with a feverish grin, Jack finally got that date he had wanted. And he had been right. They needed this.

And although she'd never admit it, he had been right about another thing. She should have gone to the dentist. But he had been wrong about one thing: it wouldn't be Fazim. It would be the corner dentist with the clinic above the local barbershop that sustained its business solely on rapidly cutting the same haircut on anybody that walked in the door. Plus, money laundering. Maybe Bjorn was in on it.

Bjorn had scrutinized the state of Leo's teeth with a disapproving frown, chiding her as though she were a misbehaving child. Something Jack agreed with but knew better than to mention during the emergency appointment.

Brown had explained how the seemingly insignificant infection had spread throughout her system, causing fever, lack of appetite, chills, and confusion. He emphasized that, if Leo had not promptly sought medical assistance, this infection could have taken a bad turn and severely compromised her health and well-being. But thankfully she had sought help before she got sepsis and went batshit crazy. He didn't use the words batshit crazy, but the medical term he used, combined with his stern tone, translated to batshit crazy.

"Would you say hearing voices would be an expected result of the infection?" she inquired apprehensively. Brown blinked twice, momentarily taken aback by the question. With a calm yet assertive tone, he responded, "Hearing voices is not an expected symptom of this infection."

"Oh. Okay. Just wondering."

"The voices are all you, babe," Jack said with an unhelpful smile.

"Miss Larsson, if you are hearing—"

"Just a general question."

Brown dipped his head, crumpled his eyebrows, and made a throaty "Hmm..." before he left to read her journal.

"What do you think?" Jack gestured in the direction of Bjorn. "Weird enough for you? Or is it still Martin forever?"

"A bit beige, but at least I get to keep my veggies."

Bjorn came back, his phone glued to his ear.

"Sorry, it's my side gig. I work as a background actor."

He muttered something incomprehensible, his attention fixed on the call, oblivious to Leo's shocked expression.

"I always play dead. It's my specialty," he finally said when the call ended. "Look." He leaned back in the chair, laying perfectly still for five minutes.

"His chest isn't even moving!" Jack whispered.

Bjorn sat up, a wide smile with what looked like extra teeth, and clapped his hands. "Well then! I had a quick call with the Peterborough clinic. They wouldn't send the journal without you signing some papers, but I might get some information from Martin. How odd is it that he is an old colleague of mine?"

"No way!"

"He is! I don't know Fazim, but based on the notes in your journal, I'd say we are better off not knowing him. He was rather pushy regarding your diet, wasn't he?"

Leo nodded, too shocked to say anything.

"Carnivore diet fan, I assume." Bjorn flung himself back into the chair, pretending to be dead again. "Dead animals, you know," he whispered without moving a single limb or lips.

"I believe we have a winner. It's not Martin, but it's definitely something," Leo said as they waited in line at the pharmacy, waiting for the magic potions Bjorn had prescribed.

"You and your dentists. I don't know anybody who's had so many strange dentists."

"What can I say? I'm a one-of-a-kind patient."

"Well." She corked her lips to the side, medicine in a green plastic bag. "I guess it's time then."

"Time for?"

"Getting my ducks in a row. Literally."

236

"Are you finally getting some help for, you know, Duckie…" Jack whispered the name.

"Yes."

"*Bye bye, Duckie.*"

42

The grand tree adjacent to the pond partially concealed the clinic's entrance, its robust branches embracing the building as if they were ancient hands cradling cherished memories. Leo envisioned how, come summer, the lush foliage would envelop the stark white walls like a hand-knitted sweater, casting soothing hues of green across the facade. The garden in which the pond was nestled was a veritable masterpiece of landscape design, expertly blending natural elements with an air of cultivated grace.

Well, this was off to a pretty good start. Leo hadn't been exactly stoked about setting foot in the clinic with its crew of quirky patients. She liked to picture herself as more of a one-time visitor, just passing through, not really one of "them." But that short, green-tinted walk up to the entrance (which was impressive, given winter's stubborn refusal to call it quits) made her feel a bit better about the whole thing.

Truth be told, she'd signed up for this adventure mostly to keep Ulrik and Jack off her back, rather than to deal with her own wants and needs. But something had changed the last week, maybe longer. `

"Could this be what growing up feels like?" she whispered, testing the echo in the glazed white room. Everything was white. Walls, tables, chairs, art. With a painful thud, her foot met resistance as it bumped into a low coffee table, barely visible in the weak contrast of the shadow on the equally white carpet.

"Welcome Leo Larsson!" A large screen at the far end of the waiting room blinked her name. *That's not ideal, from a privacy perspective,* Leo shook her head at the thought.

"Please sign in using your NFC card."

She looked down at the appointment card. Impressive. But unnecessary. Eight steps required.

One, search online for how to enable NFC on the phone.

Two, enable it.

Three, find the right angle to scan the card without the phone thinking it was being used for payment, assuming the cheapest short-range RFID was used.

Four, open the link obtained in the browser.

Five, follow the deep link to the store application.

Six, download the application.

Seven, create new login or login with SSN.

Eight, announce her arrival. Which the screen already had figured out.

Her arrival had given her ten points. And this being her first therapy appointment at the clinic gave her ten more points, the application let her know through their colorful, but creepily child-like mascot. When she had a hundred points, she could get a pan or a mediation pillow infused with lavender. She made a mental note to get the pan and hide it, as Jack had yet to understand dry-frying in a Teflon pan was not a good idea.

She sat down and waited while the room played a custom playlist, which had been created by using her journal. Another point of concern, privacy, and all, but the music wasn't too bad. Citrus and mint were misted into the air every five minutes, and each time, Leo sneezed four times. Mint allergy. Apparently not in the journal.

239

An elegant woman in her sixties swaggered in, her heels clicking like a metronome in sync with the background music.

"Larsson, Leo Larsson?"

"That's me."

The woman held out a manicured hand, and Leo shook it, surprised by the radiating warmth.

"I'm Dr. Bergstrom. Come."

They walked together down the hallway; the music following them as they left the waiting room.

"Did you like our app? We try to keep up with technology."

Not privacy laws though, Leo thought.

Green plants painted the walls green, artificial lights beaming down. The hallway smelled of something familiar. She couldn't quite place the smell, not immediately. Leo sniffed loudly.

"It's garlic. Heirloom garlic. Been in my family for generations, but my husband is not fond of garlic. Not the taste, nor the smell." She stopped, picked up a white ceramic tray and showed Leo the bulbs. "Feel free to grab a few. Artificial light and water. It's all they need."

Leo hesitated but thought of Anna and her garlic quest.

"Fermented garlic. Is that difficult to make?"

"By fermented, I assume you mean black garlic?"

Leo nodded.

"Quite easy, if you have the patience. These would be excellent candidates," she said and held a bulb against the bright light before turning her attention to Leo, examining her face. "I'm surprised Ulrik referred you to me. It has been quite a while since I've gotten a referral from across the pond," Dr. Bergstrom said as she waited for a glass door to slide open. The glass frosted as the door closed. "It pleases me," she added and went to the window, clicked on something, and looked out the window as the blinds opened, letting in the sun and the view of the pond.

"Ulrik and I were once colleagues, working together closely. However, when I decided to acquire this clinic, our opinions diverged. He didn't share my enthusiasm for embracing technology and incorporating cutting-edge advancements in the medical field." Leo hesitated, wanting to question the appropriateness of sharing such information but ultimately chose not to raise the issue. It seemed that privacy concerns hadn't been a priority when Dr. Bergstrom adopted her progressive approach to technology.

"Colleagues?" was all she said.

Dr. Bergstorm looked out the window again, waved slowly at something on the other side, a soft smile on her lips, before returning her attention to Leo.

"Shall we get started? You can call me Esther, by the way." She cast a brief, searching glance over her shoulder toward the building opposite them, her gaze settling on a round shadow at its center.

43

Meet *Zen* Leo. Well-rested, well-fed, and well-adapted Leo. Well-medicated might have something to do with all of that, but it could also be any number of things, such as three months off work, restored appetite, sleep, Jack settling on one app idea and pausing the frequent elevator pitches, or spring days flirting with summer. That one week of fantastic weather that renders Swedes nudists keen on small talk (about the weather, of course).

A small curl defied Leo's otherwise straight hair, tickling her neck like a tetchy companion. She pulled the lock taut and watched it spring back to its curly form when she let go. It bounced back, and she told herself that she would do the same. After all, one wouldn't want to be less resilient than a lock of hair, right? She cleaned up the splattered water on the sink, tossed the tissue in the bin, and left the bathroom to join her colleagues for the morning meeting, which had unironically been rescheduled for 11:45 AM. Mental elasticity—she envisioned herself bouncing back, and it felt right.

In the context of cloud architecture, elasticity is the ability to acquire resources as you need them and release resources when you no longer need them. The company had transitioned to AWS, she had learned through the general chat. The need for elastic scalability required their solution to be hosted on someone else's computers, making the shift to the cloud a mature decision. Tim had underscored this by presenting a chart illustrating their position on the cloud maturity scale, and the red dot he had used to represent the company was not even within the chart. Frederik, who had quickly identified the red dot after years of practice with various-sized dots as an Agile Coach, initially thought it was a misprint. A cloud consultant, temporarily gracing their terrestrial office with his presence, had likened the organization to a preschool filled with inexperienced children playing with containers in a back room. His analogy was not entirely off the mark. However, they didn't use containers. A precarious Lego structure would be more akin to their current masterpiece. It had taken less than two months for the greenfield project to devolve into a brownfield. A watermelon project as they had called it. Green on the outside, red on the inside.

Gerard, Hugo, and Anna waited for her, their smiles and hugs at the ready.

"Leo! You're back!" Anna flung her arms around Leo, pulling her into a tight hug and swaying her side to side. At first, Leo resisted, but her tension gradually eased with the gentle rocking. It felt incredibly good to be back.

"For you," Leo said, handing Anna a small package wrapped in parchment paper. Anna's eyes widened as she peeled back the paper.

"Garlic?" Hugo looked at Leo, wondering if her return to work had been too soon.

"Heirloom porcelain black garlic. I aged it myself," Leo announced with a proud smile, concealing the fact that Jack had been less than pleased with the electricity bill after months of running a leaky dehydrator around the clock.

Anna squealed, cupped the garlic, and inhaled the aroma. The smell had also been less than popular at home, but they had managed to ignore it, perhaps even growing to appreciate it, by the second attempt.

"You should have let it see our code; that would have aged it faster." Gerard waggled his eyebrows.

Hugo rolled his eyes at him, a playful sparkle catching the light. "Show her!"

"What?" Gerard huffed out the word.

"Your new frie—"

Anna interrupted with a white box decorated to look like the sort of box you'd get your medicine in. Inside, she revealed with a bright smile, lay hundreds of miniature cookies shaped and decorated to look like blue pills.

"Are these for Gerard?" Hugo winked. A childish jab at Gerard's age and presumed erectile dysfunction.

"Not okay, Hugo," Leo scolded Hugo with a waving finger.

"It's anti-depressants!" Anna happily announced, as if mental health was a better topic to make fun of. "Have some!"

"Gerard needs these more than Leo." Hugo pushed the box in Gerard's direction.

"First the goddamn toy, and now this. What the fuck is your problem?" Gerard's tone was firm, but the corners of his lips twitched.

"The toy?"

Gerard sighed, went to his desk, and returned with a plush toy in blue and white. A shark.

"Therapy, boss!" Hugo explained. It was unclear if the toy had been intended as a prank or sincere help, but nonetheless, the MyFirstShark1, cleverly named by a reluctant Gerard, had not been abolished to the bin. "He is going to Mexico after summer. Good to make shark friends now!"

"You are?" Mouth agape, Leo listened to Gerard as he detailed the trip to visit his uncle. The nursing home had visitors' apartments, also on the beach, and Hugo had contacts that would help him get there.

"No board shorts packed. I'm not going near the water," he reiterated.

"No sharks there, I promise." Hugo winked. "Except maybe your new friend."

"Careful, Hugo. I might tell the girls about your new hobby."

Hugo's ears turned red.

"I play Padle now," he whispered, his voice barely audible, wrapped in embarrassment and future knee injuries. He'd even gotten the twins rackets, ignoring the fact that they had the agility and coordination of a drunk raccoon.

"Let's have lunch together," Anna squeaked with pure happiness in her voice. "The cat café?"
Leo bit the inside of her chin. "No more cat café for me. Lion doesn't approve, and I feel guilty seeing other cats if he isn't okay with it."

"No polyamory-cat relationship then." Gerard laughed, referring to the poly project.

"No more poly for me." Leo winked.

"Come, it's time for company lunch!" Anna pulled Leo's arm. "Gregory and Elton brought back breakfast, moved it to lunch. You won't believe your eyes when you see what they've done with the cantina!"

In an office in the middle of the city of Gothenburg, a sparkly cantina slowly filled with people as the industrial coffee machine hummed happily in its corner. The crowd of people, who, cup in hand, lined up to fill up their caffeine-addicted bodies for a new day of work were reflected in a masterpiece of a mural. Elton had hired a local artist to create an artwork that covered the gray, large wall from top to bottom, with an ocean made from pieces of the CD's his brother had loved so much.

"They're of no good use tucked away in boxes," he had said. "It's about time they get to shine again." And with that, Elton had joined People and Culture, with his first project projecting colors and light in the room that brought people together. Not the meeting rooms, but the cantina.

"He always said the ocean was his home. And I guess it is, *Thanks to the Rolling Sea*." The crowd wasn't sure if his skills had improved in terms of speeches, but he got a round of applause for the clever, but morbid, mention of the popular song. "But I wish he'd stayed here, my home. But *That's All Right*, we'll bring a piece of the ocean, and him, here. *Viva Las Gothenburg*, and viva la *Compare the Price Price Sonic*."

"Please don't tell me that's the new company name." Gerard massaged his temples.

"It is." Hugo laughed. "You'd think Microsoft came up with that…"

44

"Are you going to miss the view?" Marie stood next to Ulrik, looking out the window. It was the last time he'd stand there, feeling the warmth of the sun rays on his face as they filtered through the green leaves, leaving a distinct pattern. Marie tapped her nails on the ledge as she waited for his reply.

"My vision is mostly indistinct shapes and hues. Nevertheless, I'm quite confident I can locate an aesthetically pleasing blur elsewhere."

"Really?" The tapping stopped. "You have to get glasses!"

"I prefer corrective contact lenses."

Marie pressed her lips into a smile and nodded. "Do you want me to carry your box as well?"

He shook his head, closed the window, and picked up the box on his desk. He expected it to be heavier, at least metaphorically, but it was light as a feather.

"That's the empty box, for the cleaners. Yours is on the chair."

The second box was not light as a feather. He grunted as he lifted the box, tightening his core like the physiotherapist had shown him. *Bend at the knees*, he reminded himself.

One box each, they walked silently down the stairs, their steps echoing goodbye against the walls.

At the entrance, Esther donned an eclectic orange suit backdropped by exotic plants. A tropical bird in her green paradise.

"Welcome to *our* clinic." She took Ulrik's box, ignoring his reluctance. "Your back, dear," she said in a hushed tone. "I absolutely love your nails, Marie. What a gorgeous color!"

Marie laughed. "I was just going to say the same about your suit!" It could be because the nails donned the same color as Esther's suit.

"Regrettably, I find myself unable to harmonize with this color palette."

"What do you think?" Esther said as they entered the clinic.

"It holds a certain charm. Given time, I suspect I could acclimate to it." He looked around, inhaling the smell of mint that had replaced the garlic. She had moved the garlic plants to the back of the clinic, far away from his office. He'd never grown to like the smell or taste of garlic. "However, I insist on retaining the verdant armchair."

"I'll let the movers know."

"And the doors."

"The doors?"

"I shall provide a more detailed account in due course," he said with a smile.

"I look forward to it." Putting down the box, Esther took hold of his arm to steady herself as she rose. She squeezed his arm. "We have a lot to talk about. I look forward to all of it."

Ulrik flashed her a radiant smile, teeth and gums on display, the creases at the corners of his eyes twinkling.

A tapping sound broke the spell.

"Are you two lovebirds done? The movers want to know where the boxes go. Chop-chop!"

45

Leo wouldn't normally have shared her medication with others, but when it came in the form of cookies, it seemed like less of a crime. Consequently, Jack received the rest of the blue cookie pills when she came home. He had always been the blue-pill type of guy. She observed the childish grin on his face, eyes large and shiny, reflecting the cookies. He took a handful, chewing with his mouth open and eyes closed, as if opening one forced the other shut, and concluded that she was the only right person for him. He gobbled down another handful, barely chewing, and hummed with satisfaction. The more annoying he became with his bottomless enthusiasm and childlike manners, the more she believed they were meant to be.

"The bank called," he later informed her. "We can start looking into buying an apartment. Probably next year, if I can establish something that resembles an income."

The funds for the startup had started trickling in, a business plan had been assembled, and Jack had masterfully put together a proof of concept. However, in its current state, it was nowhere near what the bank would consider a potential income. He had presented the startup as an established business when they had met with the bank, innocently lying like a child in a candy store.

250

"It's okay," Leo responded. "I like this apartment. We can rent for a few more years. We can still be adults."

"Adults renting an apartment?"

"Being an adult is a myth." She had heard about adulting, but in hindsight, she had never seen any examples.

Jack smacked his lips. "Or a trap."

By the window, the sun had painted the windowsill warm for Lion. He purred under the rays, undisturbed by his human slaves' lack of mortgage. He watched Jack hand Leo a *kåsa* filled with coffee before returning to his sun worshiping. The wooden drinking cup was made from birch and featured intricate patterns on the handle. Jack had bought a set of four for her birthday. That same day, the other coffee cups had vanished.

"Having these," Jack said, raising his cup in a toast, "should earn us at least a couple of adult life points. If adulthood wasn't a myth."

"What's the tally?"

"Five cheeky points."

"Well, at least they are cheeky points. Not the boring ordinary points."

"Baboon cheek points," he winked.

"Great. I had to deduct a point for that joke. Only four points as adults."

They looked out the window. Ulrik was walking Margarita, accompanied by Esther. She wore a bright yellow cardigan and cerise pants, colors contrasting Ulrik's mossy shades. She leaned against his shoulder, her head resting for a second before she pulled away, throwing her head back in what Leo presumed was a fit of laughter. Or just a fit. They looked happy.

"You know," Jack began, and Leo knew he was about to say something foolish as soon as the words left his mouth, "I'm going to need your help with the prototype app."

"Nope. No. Nein. Aldrig i livet."

"It'll be like a family business," he playfully pleaded, knowing she would ignore his entreaties.

They observed Ulrik and Esther in quietude. It seemed that Esther did most of the talking, her hands gesticulating fervently, as though they possessed a life of their own.

"You know, I appreciate the offer, but family businesses and startups just aren't my preferred brew." She lifted her *kåsa* and gestured a toast toward him. "I'd like to hold on to my sanity now that I've managed to find it."

"You'll change your mind, babe."

"I really won't."

ABOUT THE AUTHOR

Iris Classon
Software Developer, Author, Microsoft MVP, Sporty
Spice wannabe

Iris Classon is an appreciated speaker, author,
Microsoft C# MVP, and Pluralsight trainer with a
tremendous passion for programming. She has had a
remarkable career path that proves that nothing is
impossible. Switching from a licensed and registered
clinical dietician to a software developer with a dozen
certifications, applications, books, and jobs with renowned
companies. She has been featured in several newspaper
articles, online articles and podcasts such as
Hanselminutes, Computer Sweden, and Developer
Magazine. As a sought-after and frequent speaker at
conferences such as TechDays, NDC, and various user
groups she is known for her unique, creative, and uplifting
presentation style. After bragging for half a page, she
would like to say she finds the bio a tad embarrassing but
an American friend wrote it, and he says it'll help her sell
more books.

Printed in Great Britain
by Amazon